Too Much Candy and Gore

FIRST EDITION

Published in 2025 by
GREEN CAT BOOKS
19 St Christopher's Way
Pride Park
Derby
DE24 8JY

www.greencatbooks.com

ΚΟΝΤΕΝΤΣ

Dreadmoor Hall

By SL Saunders

I had been on the verge of giving up that week. After more than a decade as a paranormal investigator, the thrill had all but vanished. What had once felt like a calling had become a gimmick—reduced to cheap scares and online clout. Our little group of six still clung to relevance; we had built a decent following on social media, hosted a mildly successful podcast, and even landed a few brand deals. The merchandise sold surprisingly well, but the spark had gone.

If I'm being honest, it had been years since a genuine encounter—no whispers in the dark, no cold spots a draughty window couldn't explain, no spectral figures lurking in the shadows anymore. That is, until Dreadmoor Hall.

My once raven-black hair now bore a streak of silver I hadn't earned through age. I had seen things I couldn't explain—things I wished I could forget. I'd learned the hard way that doubt was dangerous, and belief was a blade that cut both ways. But the worst part? I'd lost one of my most trusted team members. So let me tell you about Dreadmoor Hall.

*

I adjusted my shades, making sure they fully obscured my eyes—and blocked the curious stares from too many coffee shop patrons. While waiting for my order, I kept my head down. As the main host and face of *Beyond the Static*, I was recognised more often than I liked. It didn't help that my look wasn't exactly subtle. Neither was my name.

"Ozzy! Pumpkin spice latte for one," the barista called— far too loudly for my liking.

Heads turned. Mostly women. All of them staring.

"Thanks," I muttered, snatching the paper cup with its corrugated holder and flimsy plastic lid. I turned sharply and strode out, the hem of my faux-leather coat flaring behind me as if I'd stepped out of a music video from 1987.

It would have been laughable if it had been a costume for the show—but it wasn't. This wasn't some edgy on-screen persona. This was me. Raised on a steady diet of glam rock and eyeliner, I had grown into the image naturally. I hadn't just embraced it—I had become it. Like it or not, I was every inch the namesake my mum had saddled me with. And honestly? I didn't mind.

The shop windows were already dressed for the season, adorned with plump orange pumpkins and leaves in shades of burnt amber and earthy brown. Some displays went the spooky route—skeletons grinning behind glass, ghouls mid-screech—while others catered to the Instagram crowd, with perfectly arranged hay bales and cosy flannel aesthetics. Autumn was in the air. I could feel it in the crisp bite of the wind and smell it in the sweet, spiced steam curling up from my latte.

I was about to cut through the local cemetery—a well-worn shortcut from one end of town to my flat—when the shrill ring of my phone snapped me out of my autumn reverie. I didn't need psychic powers to guess who it was. The screen lit up with 'Jenny, your *ghoulie PA*.'

"Hey, Jen. How's it going? Anything new come in?" I asked, though I already suspected the answer was yes. Jen didn't call without reason.

"Well, Oz," she said, a mischievous giggle sounding down the phone, "funny you should ask. We've had an inquiry—Dreadmoor Hall. It's a big one. We'll need the full team. And the pay's decent too."

Dreadmoor Hall. The name rang a bell, but I couldn't place it. Why?

"Brilliant, Jen. Call them back and confirm the details. I'll check in at the office in an hour." Jen's cheery voice signed off with a "speak soon," and the line went dead.

I tugged my scarf tighter around my neck and took a long swig of my coffee, letting the warmth and spice jolt my senses awake. I needed to be sharp—there was research to do back at the office. Whenever a job came in, we dug deep before setting foot on site. That was rule number one. My old mentor had drilled it into me early on: never go in blind. Know your house, and, more importantly, know its history.

Before heading to the office, I had to stop by home to pick up what some might have called one of the most important members of our team—though not officially on the payroll, at least not in cash. Her payment came in the form of treats and kisses on the head. The moment my key turned in the lock, I heard the familiar sound of claws scrambling across the laminate floor. I braced myself. As soon as the door opened, there she was—Sabbra, my loyal German Shepherd—launching herself at me with all the joy and enthusiasm only a dog could give.

She had been more than a pet. She was family—and on investigations, she was often the first to sense what the rest of us couldn't.

"Hey, Sabbs, want to come to work with me? Food first, of course—then we'll walk to the office and meet up with the gang."

She was already in the kitchen before I got there, sitting patiently by her bowl. Sabbra was well trained, sharp as ever, and deeply intuitive. She loved being part of the team. I doubted she saw it as work—more like an adventure.

Every location had been a new world to explore, and she had treated it that way—sniffing into corners we couldn't reach. When something unseen lingered in the air, her hackles would rise before any of us even felt the chill. She hadn't just been a loyal companion. Sabbra had been a guard dog in every sense of the word—both physical and spiritual. I packed her bag with plenty of treats—though she had her own stash at the office too, being a regular. She even had a bed tucked into a quiet corner—her little base of operations.

I slipped on her coat—the one with the reflective strips—as the air had already taken on a noticeable bite with the late afternoon creeping in. Her tail wagged contentedly as we headed out for a short walk—twenty minutes, just enough to stretch our legs before the team meeting about Dreadmoor Hall.

I had chosen offices tucked away in the old part of town, and, truth be told, I had much preferred it to the newer developments. That area had a soul. The architecture hadn't been sleek or modern—it had been a beautiful chaotic blend of 14th to 17th-century styles. Mediaeval stonework sat beside Gothic arches; Renaissance flourishes met Georgian symmetry. The streets had felt like walking through a timeline, every building whispering its history.

As I had approached our office, its dark, brooding silhouette had come into view. The building had looked like something lifted straight from a Victorian ghost story—tall and narrow, with pointed-arch windows framed by crumbling stone. Iron sconces had flanked the heavy oak door, and ivy had crawled up the exterior like green veins on ancient skin. The blackened roof had sloped steeply, crowned with jagged finials, and the stained glass above the entrance had shimmered faintly with whatever light the grey afternoon had offered.

It didn't just house a paranormal investigation team—it *looked* the part.

I had known Jen would've already gathered the rest of the team. Most of them had lived just a stone's throw from the office—another reason we had chosen that location, aside from the fantastic Gothic aesthetic.

Matteus had probably been there for hours. He was our tech specialist, aka the man in the chair, completely obsessed with scouring every minute sound captured on the audio recorders. He had spent entire afternoons holed up in the office, replaying old investigations just to make sure he hadn't missed a whisper.

I had suspected he also liked being close to his gear. His apartment was far too small to house it all now, and over time, the office had become more of a tech lab than a workspace. The place was packed with high-end monitors, infrared and full-spectrum cameras, audio recorders, EMF detectors, REM pods—and one of my personal favourites, the spirit box. We'd started with just the basics, but now... I couldn't even name half the equipment we had.

"Boo," came a voice behind me just as I reached for the office door—followed by a familiar squeal of delight.

"Can you believe we've got a booking at Dreadmoor

Hall?" Carmen enquired, grinning at me, her energy as infectious as ever.

"I know. Ready to help me research?" I asked and returned her smiled. "I'm hitting a wall—memory blocks or something. Feels psychic, but I can't figure out why."

Carmen leaned in, scanning my face with her usual, uncomfortably close intensity.

"Hmm... let's see what we uncover once those computers are fired up, baby," she said, linking her arm through mine. "If that Hall's hiding dark secrets, you *know* we'll find them."

Carmen had always been a gifted psychic and one hell of a researcher. Paired with my skill set, we made a formidable team.

She was also one of my closest friends—and sometimes, we'd crossed the line between friendship and something more. We never talked about it. Never needed to.

Carmen Celeste—always a mystery. She'd had a knack for making me laugh, for keeping the mood light even when things got dark. She claimed that was her real name, but we'd all teased her, saying it sounded made-up.

Her comeback had always been, "Like Ozzy is real?" She'd had a point. My mum really had named me Ozzy.

"Glad you two are here. Come and have a look at the

layout and photos of Dreadmoor Hall I pulled from the historical archives," Billy called, beckoning us over to his monitor before we'd even had the chance to shut the door behind us.

Sabbra padded off towards her usual corner once I unclipped her lead. She circled her bed before settling down with a low huff. It was as if she sensed the storm coming—the calm before the chaos, as always.

Billy was officially our historian, though, to be fair, we all wore multiple hats. Field notes, interviews, background checks—whoever was available stepped up. That was the beauty of our team: no ego, no fuss—just the work.

As if on cue, the final member of our crew appeared from the kitchen, balancing a tray of drinks.

"Usual for everyone," River said with a grin. Their smile was as warm as their energy—light, grounding, and utterly contagious.

River was our all-rounder, but they had a real knack for visuals. They made sure we looked the part for the camera and practically lived in charity shops, hunting for pieces that matched our on-screen personas. You *could* even say they curated our 'costumes'—stylised versions of who we were, just turned up a notch for the audience.

"Cheers, River," echoed around the room as we each took our drinks.

"Looks like an impressive place, Billy," I said, eyeing the old black-and-white photo on his screen. "We're gonna need the full kit for this one."

Billy nodded, but a shadow passed across his expression.

"Yeah... and I found something else," he said, tapping a file open on his desktop. "A newspaper article from 1972. Headline read: 'Dreadgore Hall'."

"Dreadgore?" Carmen echoed, raising an eyebrow.

"Yeah," Billy continued. "Four members of the same family had been found murdered there on Halloween— mutilated. The case was never solved. Police had suspected the father, but nothing was ever proven. Locals always claimed he'd been possessed... something about a demonic presence in the cellar."

The room fell quiet. Even Sabbra lifted her head slightly, her ears twitching.

"Well," I muttered, my fingers tightening around the warm mug, "guess we weren't just chasing cold spots and creaky floorboards this time."

"When the booking came through for tonight, the owners of Dreadmoor Hall apologised for the short notice," Jen explained, pulling up the email. "They said three paranormal investigation teams had already pulled out on them. I thought that was a bit odd—and honestly, quite unprofessional—when I first spoke to them."

"Sounds more like paranoia," Matteus muttered, turning his laptop towards us. He'd just uploaded a thread from a paranormal forum about Dreadmoor.

I leaned in, scanned the screen, then started reading some of the entries aloud.

Don't go to Dreadmoor Hall—an investigation team went there in the late 1970s, and all four members ended up in psychiatric care.

Another post read: *My friend visited someone at Dreadmoor in 1980 and got possessed by the Devil.*

Most of the entries followed the same tone—urban legends, maybe, or exaggerated local lore—but a thread of dread ran through all of them.

Carmen pointed to one further down the page. "Have you seen this one?"

We all leaned closer as she read aloud:

"If you go into Dreadmoor Hall to investigate, at least one of you won't come out alive."

Silence settled over the room. Even the usual background hum of equipment seemed to fade. I wasn't sure whether to let out a mock-ghoulish laugh or take it deadly seriously—until Jen broke the tension with a grin.

"Well, that explained why we got the gig over the SAU," she said. "Looks like they wussed out."

The Spectral Analysis Unit considered themselves the elite in our region—always polished, always clinical. In my experience, they didn't walk away from a case like this unless they had a damn good reason. But with such short notice, I hadn't had time to delve into why they really pulled out.

We only had a couple of hours before we were due to head out to Dreadmoor Hall. Billy and Matteus were already loading the van with gear, Carmen and Jen had gone to collect the food we'd ordered, and River was flitting around the office, laying out our outfits for the shoot—making sure every look matched our curated paranormal personas, all very gothic-looking.

Sabbra stared up at me with those big, soulful, chocolate-brown eyes.

"Come on, girl," I said, grabbing her lead. "One quick walk before the chaos began."

The night had already fallen, cloaking the streets in a deep indigo sky. It wasn't Halloween yet—still the weekend before—but the festivities had begun. Kids in plastic fangs and superhero capes paraded into community centres for parties. Groups of drunken twenty-somethings laughed too loudly as they stumbled towards pubs, women dressed in vampy costumes with heels too high, and men in cartoon onesies pretending to be Shaggy and Scooby.

I took a deep breath, letting the cool air fill my lungs. The sharp autumn bite in the breeze grounded me—just for a moment—before I stepped into whatever musty darkness awaited us beneath Dreadmoor Hall. I always got the jitters before an investigation. Not the kind you could laugh off, either. These weren't just ghost stories to me, or some viral internet spoof for clicks. *I believed, or rather, I had in the past.*

The owners of Dreadmoor had mentioned part of the Hall was being hired out that night for a combined Halloween and 18th birthday party—but they assured us our investigation would remain confined to the cellar and the uninhabited, older wing of the building.

My phone buzzed with a message: *Food's here.*

"Come on, girl," I said to Sabbra. "Let's fill our stomachs before dealing with any spectral entities."

Takeaway nights had always been a highlight at the office. No matter what chaos we were preparing for, those moments reminded me how lucky I was. We weren't just colleagues—we were a family.

Years of working together had bonded us in ways only shared fear, wonder, and adrenaline could. Because how could you explain to someone that a spirit box had clearly said the name of your teammate standing right beside you—and know, without a doubt, that it hadn't been a setup or a hoax just to boost views or go viral on YouTube?

We'd lived through things together—real things. Like the time a heavy wooden chair had slid across the floor, unaided, during a vigil. Or when a ghostly orb had flickered on the full-spectrum camera, and the room had dropped ten degrees in an instant. The hairs on the backs of our hands had risen in unison more times than I could count. We hadn't needed convincing. We believed—because we'd seen it for ourselves.

After we'd eaten, there were still a few last-minute things to prepare before we headed out to Dreadmoor Hall.

Billy stepped back into the office, brushing a bit of drizzle off his coat. "Matteus is in the van—it's all packed and ready to go. I'll ride with him. Jen, are you coming with us?"

Jen was already reaching for her coat, trying—and failing—not to look too eager. It wasn't exactly a secret that she had a soft spot for Billy. That left River to drive me, Carmen, and Sabbra.

As we pulled up to Dreadmoor Hall, the first thing to greet us was a pair of tall, wrought-iron gates, flanked by stone pillars weathered by time and tangled with ivy. They groaned open with a reluctant screech, revealing a long, winding driveway. The Hall itself loomed at the top of the incline; half shrouded in mist—a monstrous silhouette etched against the darkening sky. I shuddered at its sheer scale.

From somewhere inside, music echoed—muted bass thudding through the stone walls—while coloured lights spilt from one of the lower rooms, casting flickers of movement across the grounds. Oversized, grotesque Halloween inflatables swayed awkwardly in the breeze, and cheerful *Happy 18th* banners fluttered along the hedgerows. It wasn't hard to guess where the party was being held.

Oddly, the decorations took some of the edge off the Hall's foreboding presence—but not all of it. The structure still loomed, dark and ancient, as if watching us... and waiting. Jen was already on the phone with our host by the time we pulled up—it was easier to call than to stand outside, ringing a bell and hoping someone would answer in this towering goliath of a hall. We waited patiently for her to appear, unloading our gear as we did—ready to distribute it once we were inside.

A strikingly attractive woman emerged from the arched stone entrance. Tall and poised, with dark hair cascading over her shoulders, she wore a black velvet Gothic dress paired with knee-high boots. I had to admit; she looked like she'd stepped out of the pages of a Victorian ghost story. If Gothic elegance were the unspoken dress code, she'd absolutely nailed it.

"Hello, and welcome to you all," she said with a smooth, practised smile. "I'll be your host this evening—Mrs Bainbridge, current owner of Dreadmoor Hall."

We smiled politely, and Matteus and Billy offered awkward murmurs of hello.

"Follow me, please," Mrs Bainbridge said, turning gracefully on her heel. "I'll show you where you should set up first, then give you a briefing on what has been happening—and why we are needing your help."

I'd learned it was best to hold off on questions until the host had guided us to the investigation area. That way, we usually got their full attention without distraction—especially in places as vast and imposing as this.

As we followed her inside, I couldn't help but notice the stark contrast within the Hall. Some areas had been beautifully preserved, oozing historical charm, while others clearly cried out for renovation. The grandeur was undeniable, but so was the sense of neglect in certain corners—like forgotten chapters in an otherwise elegant tale.

We passed several teenagers in the corridor—laughing loudly, clearly fuelled by alcohol, and utterly unconcerned by whispered tales of ghosts or the alleged online killer linked to Dreadmoor Hall.

"I'll be letting you set up in the cellar," Mrs Bainbridge said, her voice calm and deliberate. "That's where I believe most of the activity is coming from."

I watched her closely as she spoke. She carried herself with a composed, almost aloof air—cool and collected, as if none of it rattled her in the slightest. But I knew better. People rarely called us in without some level of fear. First though, we needed to hear her full story.

Carmen had been watching Mrs Bainbridge too—or rather, watching my reaction to her.

"She's quite attractive, isn't she?" she said, a teasing edge in her voice. I knew Carmen well enough to hear what she wasn't saying. She was probing, as always, testing the waters for something else. I kept it professional, shrugging with a faint smile. "Hadn't noticed, to be honest. I was more in awe of the building... the architecture."

Carmen narrowed her eyes and gave her usual close-up scan of my face, as if searching for cracks in my expression. I felt my cheeks grow warm under her intensity.

Then, suddenly, she stopped.

Her head tilted slightly. "There's something here... it's cold," she whispered—and then her gaze glazed over, her body going unnaturally still as she slipped into a trance. Sabbra responded too—her hackles raised as she stood firm, growling low at the doorway ahead.

River crouched beside her, giving her a reassuring pat. "It's all right, girl. Stay calm." Then, turning to the others, she added, "Matteus, get the camera ready. Billy, grab the rest of the equipment." River always kept her cool when things started to feel real.

Mrs Bainbridge was speaking quietly with Jen, explaining that the very door Sabbra had reacted to—the one Carmen had frozen in front of—was the entrance to the cellar. It was down there, she said, that the most intense activity had been reported. I stepped closer, watching Carmen's motionless form.

"Mrs Bainbridge, we need to wait until Carmen comes out of her trance before we proceed," I said firmly. "Whatever she's seeing right now could be crucial. Her visions have led us before—she'll tell us what's waiting down there."

Mrs Bainbridge gave a silent nod.

Carmen groaned, her eyes fluttering as she came out of the trance. Her voice was shaky, almost pleading.

"Mustn't go down there... mustn't go down there. One of you isn't coming out of here alive."

She looked pale—visibly shaken. I instinctively wrapped an arm around her, trying to reassure her.

"It's all right," I whispered.

"No—you don't understand," she said, pulling back. "One of us is going to die."

I tried to keep things grounded. "Hey, are you sure you weren't just spooked by that forum post earlier? It was the same message, remember?"

She shrugged off my arm, eyes wide with fear.

"No! One of us is going to die tonight! What part of that don't you understand? There's something down there... something evil. Truly evil. I'm not going into that cellar. We never should've come here. Now I understand why the SAU backed out—they weren't being cowardly. They were saving themselves."

I'd never seen Carmen like this before—and looking back, I should have listened to her.

"Okay, look," I said gently, trying to meet her halfway, "if you want to sit this one out, that's fine. Go grab a drink at the party. Stay where it's busy and safe, and with people."

She looked at me—really looked at me—and for a moment, I saw something desperate in her eyes. Then she exhaled, almost defeated.

"All right. Yeah, you're right. I'm just... spooked from the post and tired. I'll grab a drink and maybe join you in ten."

The moment Mrs Bainbridge opened the cellar door, a sudden drop in temperature hit us like a wave.

"Did you get that temperature drop, Billy?" Matteus asked, glancing at the screen of the handheld device.

"Yeah," Billy replied, eyes wide. "That was insane—definitely recorded a drop of several degrees."

Sabbra darted ahead of us, bounding down into the cellar and sniffing the corners with intense focus.

River tugged their collar up around their neck. "Damn, it's freezing in here... and it smells like dried blood. Yuk."

I stood in the centre of the first room, the spirit box humming in my hands. The static crackled with anticipation. Mrs Bainbridge gestured for Billy and Matteus to begin setting up. "This is the room where most of the activity has been reported," she said quietly.

"I knew it," River muttered, wrinkling their nose. "It reeks of blood in here."

For the first time, Mrs Bainbridge's confident demeanour slipped. A shadow of discomfort passed over her face.

"You're correct," she whispered. "This is the room where my relatives were murdered... in 1972."

I decided to step in. "You said you're struggling with entities now, and that's why you called us. You also mentioned trying other paranormal teams before us. What exactly do you believe is the issue? Online forums have accused the father of the murder victims—what was his relation to you?"

Mrs Bainbridge shifted uncomfortably under my questioning, but digging into the difficult details is part of any serious investigation. If we want answers, we have to press. Before she could respond, the static from the spirit box crackled louder—and then clear words cut through the noise. Billy immediately hit record.

"Murder... Tom... murder... Tom... killed them all... Four ...cold blood... possessed... one of you will die... Carmen... death to Carmen."

Then, just as suddenly as it started, the box went silent.

A dark shadow shot across the room.

"Oh my God, did you see that?" Jen cried, eyes wide, her voice sharp with panic.

"I'm hoping I caught it on camera," Billy muttered to Matteus, already fiddling with his rig. "I'll check the footage back at the office during the tech analysis.

River, eyes locked on the retreating shadow, moved fast toward the far cellar doorway—Sabbra bounded after them, alert and growling low.

"Hey, guys," River called out, glancing back. "Did someone lock the cellar door behind us when we came in?"

The question hit me like a stone in the gut.

"I didn't," I said.

Mrs Bainbridge shook her head, pale and silent.

I turned to her, my voice tight. "Talk. Quickly. Who is Tom?"

She trembled, her composure starting to slip.

"He's my dad... the man accused and acquitted of murdering my two brothers, sister and mum in this very room."

My stomach dropped. The next question sat like ice on my tongue, but I had to ask it.

"Where is he now?" She sank to her knees, eyes brimming with tears.

"He... he still lives here." I nearly shouted the next words, though some part of me already knew the answer.

"Does he have a key to the cellar?"

Mrs Bainbridge covered her face with her hands and sobbed, unable to speak.

Suddenly, the spirit box crackled to life again.

The music from the party upstairs faded—distorted and distant now, like a memory unravelling. Then a voice cut through the static, warped but unmistakably Carmen's, as if echoed from somewhere far away:

"Ozzy... one of us is going to die tonight."

The air grew heavy. The blood drained from my face as I

dropped to the cold stone floor, heart pounding.

Outside, police and ambulance sirens screamed through the night.

The White Lady and the Headless Knight

By Kram Rednip

'Ah yes, I forgot to tell you, Annabelle, but sometimes Adrienne appears.'

'Adrienne? Who's she?'

'The first occupant of the manor, who died in childbirth in 1840, she appears from time to time, then disappears again.'

****

'The thing is: do we exist, or don't we? It's a very pertinent question, you know.'

Adrienne, the White Lady of Massingham Manor, sighed that plaintive, whispering sigh of hers that was formerly so effective in persuading living beings that she *did* exist, on encountering her for the first time at the top of her staircase. But Sir Clovis, the Headless Knight, was having none of it.

'Oh tush,' he responded, 'don't come over all Hamlet with me. Our sole objective is to convince our human friends that we *do* exist. We do it in different ways, of course; with you, it's soft and gentle, unexpected appearances on the staircase, the rustling of white fabric, the plaintive moan and then you're gone, leaving them open-mouthed and wondering. With me it's more brutal. I just confront them when they're crossing a bridge or whatever, bloody head tucked under arm, and scare them witless.'

The White Lady sighed once again. Really, she thought, the Headless Knight could certainly be rather brutal in expressing his sentiments. Understandable, of course, as a human being himself he had met his end as an English man-at-arms at the Battle of Castillon in 1453, decapitated at a single stroke by the French Chevalier de la Breze du Garde de Chateauvallon. He'd been bitter about it ever since, no doubt reflecting that if le Chevalier had had his wits about him, he'd have captured him and ransomed him for a handsome profit, rather than just slicing him in two with his great broadsword to no profit whatsoever.

'You don't understand what I mean, Clo-Clo,' she replied (all spectres have pet nicknames between themselves). 'I know we need to make those humans *think* we exist, but do we, really? We don't *actually have* physical form after all, we're just chimerae that come and go as it pleases us, to appear or not, so even if they *think* we're real we're perhaps actually no more than fleeting visions that we somehow project into their brains... a sort of artificial intelligence, in fact...I just don't know.'

The Headless Knight snorted contemptuously. Not that easy to snort contemptuously, when your head is detached from the rest of you... but still. The White Lady persisted.

'On the whole, however, I think we probably *do* exist. We have thoughts, and even feelings, just like living people, don't we? So yes, I think we're probably real after all.'

The White Lady certainly had a very 'real', pragmatic mindset, for a phantom. In general, she was quite Cartesian in her reasoning.

****

'This is all very well,' the Headless Knight reflected, 'but it doesn't get over the fact that both of us... we're a bit dated, a bit... predictable, one might say. Take yourself for example, Adri. I mean... a White Lady! Just think how many spectral White Ladies there are in the world, why, there must be dozens and dozens of them! Not surprising if the effects of your appearances are a little... underwhelming. And even me, I count on the shock factor as you know, but I've noticed recently that the living are becoming a little blasé about my manifestations. Why, only the other day, when I popped out on my bridge at Montford in front of that family, the little boy actually *laughed at me*! And I'm pretty sure that the father said something rather contemptuous, even if I didn't catch exactly what it was. And you said the same thing, when you appeared at the top of the staircase in your Manor the last time, the children were a little frightened at first but then their mother told them there was nothing to worry about, they were quite used to you showing up like that, they hardly noticed you anymore.'

Another plaintive sigh from The White Lady.

'Yes... you're quite right, Clo-Clo, as always. And afterwards, when I manifested in front of them again, they didn't even look up from their iPads and smartphones... it really was most frustrating.'

'Most unfortunate. Of course, we can't change from what we are – you'll always be a White Lady, me always a Headless Knight – but perhaps we need to think about changing our approach a little.'

'What exactly do you mean?'

'Well, we could integrate ourselves more into the *modern* world of the living, instead of just sticking slavishly to our traditional practices; me appearing on my bridge all the time, you at the top of your staircase, or wherever. It's all just too dated. And peoples' attention spans are so short nowadays, we just need to think of new ways of grabbing that attention, if they're not going to think of us as just some kind of clever hologram generated by the internet, or artificial intelligence...'

****

A day or two later, little Annabelle was wandering about in the garden in front of the manor. It was a lovely spring day, the trees were in leaf, the flowers in bloom, but... Annabelle had her nose buried in her smartphone, totally absorbed in her video game.

A 'ping' came through on the smartphone, announcing arrival of a text message. Mechanically, Annabelle paused her game and switched to her textbox.

'Hi Annabelle, your new friend, Adri, here. Listen, I've something quite important to tell you. Now that I've gone digital, I can put you in the way of quite a few things that might be of interest to you.'

However, Annabelle *wasn't* interested. Already bored by the text messages she'd been receiving from 'her new friend Adri' the last few days, she didn't even bother to reply, just returned to her game. She needed to concentrate hard. The game concerned a feisty princess called Bella who had to navigate her way through the Amethyst Jungle, avoiding the attentions of the Evil Magician, Anthrax, and various malevolent wild monsters of his who tried to ambush her and gobble her up, along the way. She had some friendly little will-o'-the wisp fairies to help her, but frankly they weren't up to much. Despite Annabelle's best efforts the feisty princess got gobbled up, for the umpteenth time.

Another 'ping!' came through.

'Sorry, Annabelle, I know I'm a bother, but it's me again. You know what? I was thinking of how your brother, Rodolphe, hacked into your X account the other day, how cross you were about it. Well, I know a way you could get back at him. All you need to do is...'

With a snarl of contempt, Annabelle deleted all the

dozen or so messages she'd received from Adri over the last two days, then tagged her as 'undesirable' in her mailbox. Then without another thought about it she returned to her game, setting Bella skipping yet again along the Cornelian Path into the Amethyst Jungle, to lock horns with Anthrax and his horrible monsters.

****

'So tell me, Adri – how've you been getting on with those tiresome children? Grabbing their attention a little more now, are you? You see, I told you things would take a turn for the better if you acquired a Spectral Smartphone...'

Adrienne snorted, being not at all in the mood to listen to Sir Clovis's brand of airy flippancy.

'Oh, just shut up, you headless moron! Things *have not* taken a turn for the better! I did what you said, intercepted them whenever they're absorbed with their smartphones – which is most of the time, it must be said – but the effect was just the same as before. Got their attention for perhaps a millisecond, then they just went on with whatever BotChat they were having, whatever computer game they were playing. Especially that little beast Annabelle, with her Amethyst Jungle and Anthrax the Evil Magician, and what have you.'

Sir Clovis was truly mortified. He would have shaken his head in sympathy, but... well, you probably understand why he couldn't do that.

'But, Adri… Adri, *darling*… I'm sure you'd have more impact if only you persist a little more. You see… it's all very well to distract them, but the way to *really* grab their attention is to get right into whatever they are preoccupied with, rather than try to divert them from it. Take me, for example, I've been having really an amazing amount of success, since we last spoke. I've become quite a… quite an *Influencer* I think the term is, with a very large following on Instagram and Facebook…'

'Oh, cut the crap, you old fool! I'd say you'd lost your head, if you hadn't already done so in 1453! I don't believe you've made any more progress that I have in getting noticed…'

The Headless Knight winced – he could still do that – he'd never seen Adrienne as angry as this before.

'Calm down, Adri, calm down! I really don't mean to provoke you! But it's really quite easy. Step one: divvy up your identity. With me, well, since my chief weapon is horror, I decided to go gothic. So then step two: I inveigled myself into all sorts of gothic websites and blogs and things and started to build up a following. Then step three: I set up an Instagram account and a Facebook page of my own, and a WhatsApp group, and things just… well, they really just took off from there. I've got thousands and thousands of followers now, just hanging on my every word…'

The White Lady opened her mouth to say something

sarcastic, but Sir Clovis cut her short.

'And then step four: move back into the real, as well as the virtual World. Me, I set up a gothic heavy metal progressive rock band – I'm the bassist, you know – we call ourselves the Tadpoles of Death and we're already booked to play at Hellfest, and the Metallica Megablast, and a host of other venues besides. We're bringing out an album next year. I really wow them when my head slips off and rolls across the stage foaming at the mouth.'

He placed his virtual hand gently on her virtual arm.

'Of course, I'm not suggesting anything so extreme in your case. With you, the soft and gentle touch should be enough. You should try it out with your pesky children. Just get inside their heads – which really means getting inside whatever virtual reality vibe they're indulging in at any given time – and you'll see what a difference it makes.'

Adrienne was not really convinced, but she decided to take Clo-Clo's advice just the same. The truth is, she was becoming a little desperate. And maybe she wanted to be able to prove him wrong, just so she could bawl him out a little more.

****

Annabelle was having a few problems in the Amethyst Jungle. Bella was beset on all sides by Anthrax's malevolent monsters, and the will-o'-the-wisp fairies, though loyally trying to help her, were being extinguished one by one with just a 'puff' and a whimper. It wouldn't be long before Bella herself was extinguished, as always.

Suddenly, what looked like nothing more than a large white blob appeared on the screen from nowhere. Dashing about the jungle, it confronted each monster in turn and extinguished each of *them* too. They expired with a ghastly moan in a puff of black smoke. Hooray! Suddenly Bella's path towards the Crystal Castle was clear. The white blob cleared the way before her, smashing any remaining malevolent monsters into the undergrowth either side of the Cornelian Path. Bella flung herself into the arms of Horatio, the Handsome Prince of the Happy Way, at last.

The white blob burst over Bella and the Handsome Prince in an ecstatic firework-display of victory. Swirling around, expanding, it transformed into The White Lady of Massingham Manor, flying through the air, her long hair streaming out behind her. *Congratulations, Annabelle! With my help, you've overcome the evil intentions of Anthrax the Dark Magician! Now, if you stay with me, we can move on to Level 4 of 'Bella in the Amethyst Jungle'. Just log into my website:*
(dameblanche.com@manoirmagique)
and I'll give you lots of hints and tips on how to proceed! And don't worry – I'll be with you, all the way!

****

'So – you took my advice – and it worked out in the end?'

'Yes, Clo-Clo, everything has worked out fine. I keep getting messages from Annabelle every time we make it up to a new level in the Amethyst Jungle: *"OMG! Thanx White Lady! You're just wonderful, big kisses"* stuff like that, with lots of little… mojos, or emojis, I think they're called.'

'You see? I told you it would be fine if you just persisted. What are your plans, now?'

'Well, like you, I'm on Facebook and Instagram, I have quite a following, don't think I could classify myself as an 'influencer' like you just yet, though… but I've started working on the other children, Suzanne, Marion, Simone, and even that odious little beast, Rodolphe, who is completely obsessed with horrible gangster games and violence. You should have a go at him yourself, you know; he's just the right type for your brand of Rocky Horror Show stuff.'

Sir Clovis was very, very pleased, and not a little relieved. He'd always had a soft spot for The White Lady, thinking that if he'd remained intact and if she'd lived in the 15th century rather than the 19th he would have wooed her with all the medieval chivalric courtly love that had been so much part of him before Castillon. He'd been genuinely hurt by her savage response to his initial suggestions, and now he told her so.

'Yes, Clo-Clo, I'm sorry about that, I know I can over-react at times, but don't worry, we'll always be very, very good friends. And you know, all this has set me thinking again about what I was saying that time about existence and reality, whether we spectres are real or not...'

Sir Clovis sighed; he wasn't much of a philosopher himself; thinking too hard brought on one of his headaches.

'You mean: *"to be or not to be, that is the question"*: that kind of stuff?'

'Exactly so. If you remember, I'd sort of concluded that we *are* real, that we *do* exist. And now, in parallel alongside our *spectral* existence, we have our *virtual* existence, which adds another interesting dimension to things. And it certainly helps us achieve recognition: it seems that for many humans nowadays virtual reality is more real than actual corporeal reality. Take little Annabelle, for instance; she spends as much time as she can with her nose buried in her smartphone, so the 'make-believe' of the Amethyst Jungle has become the 'real-believe' at the core of her existence. I don't think she knows the difference anymore.'

Clo-Clo's head, clutched tightly under one arm, was starting to throb. He loved his White Lady dearly, but this was a bit too much.

'Anyway, what troubles me a little about... about this new direction we're taking, is that it just encourages the humans – particularly the susceptible ones, like

Annabelle – to go too far down that path of alternative reality. As we've seen so many times, it can be very, very dangerous. We need to think hard about that, and then perhaps do what we can to… to jerk them back towards their actual physical world so there's a better balance in their lives between the two.'

Sir Clovis closed his eyes tightly.

'Yes, Adri, I think I understand; in part at least. You're so much more… so much more sensitive than I am. Sounds as if you're about to embark on some kind of a crusade, again! Well, I'm with you all the way. As you know I'm your loyal servant for always and always, your *'parfit gentil knight'* if I can borrow the term from my old friend Geoffrey Chaucer, and very familiar with the concept of crusades besides. So, if you're needing a little shock factor in "jerking them back" as you put it, I'm definitely your champion. Just point me in the right direction, and I'll know what to do.'

****

Ah yes, crusades… it wasn't straightforward, as Adrienne found out when she tried to ease Annabelle back towards taking some interest in the real world around her rather than the virtual one embedded in her smartphone and her iPad. But little by little, she succeeded. Annabelle had indeed come to regard her as her friend, who could help her not just with winning her computer games, but in coming to terms with the realities (that word again!) and the dangers that were all around but that she had never taken much notice of before. She was at that age when a little girl (or little boy, for that matter) starts to ask lots of questions of her(him)self, and perhaps needs someone to rely on to help her answer those questions and… negotiate her way through her own Amethyst Jungle, as one might say.

Unfortunately, Annabelle's parents were not much help in all of this. They were busy, working people with their own concerns, often too tired and irritable to pay much attention to their children's psychological needs, and willing enough to let them play away endlessly on their smartphones in order to have a little peace. In short, they had their own, adult, alternative realities; and if the White Lady found this somewhat deplorable, she was at something of a loss as to what to do about it.

In the end, she called on the support of her *fidele serviteur,* the Headless Knight. Being rather more up-front than she was, but just as resourceful, he soon dreamed up one or two ways to jolt Annabelle's mum and dad into a state in which they themselves would be capable of taking over the role of steering their dear children safely through puberty and into the *relatively* safe haven of young adulthood. He has only just begun his shock treatment, but initial results are very promising; and we have every confidence that he will succeed, in the end.

The Long Way Home

By Neil Pettifer

....

We human beings are so convinced of our mastery over this planet, but beneath our sturdy buildings and smooth tarmac roads, this world still has jaws and teeth.

....

Greenhill Lane in Halestown was a very desirable place to live. The looping road begins with a lavish sign and is nestled at the quiet end of Halestown high street. The residents of Greenhill Lane had eagerly donated towards upgrading their street sign from the council-issued one to a rather modern-looking silver plate. A little way past this impressive signage, a healthy stretch of greenery swooped gently around the 130 properties that called Greenhill Lane home. These homes were occupied by the type of families who valued a quiet and peaceful neighbourhood. Even the wider community of Halestown appeared to be a picturesque settlement littered with quaint shops and a quietly reserved sense of pride.

The residents of this little haven had every right to be proud, having earned themselves a respectable 4th position in the 2025 publication of 'Top 100 places to live in England'. This achievement rippled through the community, instilling everyone with a sense of comfort in their surroundings. Neighbours, who knew little more than each other's first name, would feel it only right to offer a "good morning" and even compliment each other on a "fantastic lawn" or a "well-groomed rose bush".

Like many great works of art, Greenhill Lane is not without its imperfections. While the tarmac on the road is smooth and dark and the kerbs are kept remarkably clean, the road itself is split by an alleyway which cracks down the spine of the street weaving behind back gardens and running almost from one end of the road to the other.

This route had no real benefits for the residents, it was a marginally quicker track, but most passers-by were put off by the smell. There was no garden access down there and if there ever had been, the neighbourhood had long since blocked it up, preferring to conceal the unsightly path by growing voluptuous trees and bushes at the ends of their gardens. If the occasional mischievous youngster was caught skulking around the alley, they were usually spotted and shooed away by the nearest neighbour who would bang on their window and frighten them off. The older children would swap stories and rumours about people going missing down there. They would dare each other to cut down the forbidden route and, every once in a while, one of them would head boldly into the passage. Sometimes they would emerge with pale faces and swear blind that they'd seen something in the gloom of the alleyway, or they would insist that their watch had suddenly stopped working. These strange occurrences, though inexplicable, were a great source of entertainment.

Besides the perilous lure of this overgrown trail, the only other threat to Greenhill Lane's impeccable setting was a highly unsavoury lady now living at number 37. This old woman's property had been empty for a year until, much to the dismay of the neighbours, she had moved in almost overnight. There had been no removal vans or supportive family lugging furniture in or out of the house or even a "For sale" sign. "Loopy Lilly", as the neighbourhood kids had labelled her, simply showed up one day and shut herself inside number 37. She rarely seemed to leave and if anyone approached, she quickly retreated back inside her house mumbling to herself. Nervous about the damage a character like this could do to their "Fourth most desirable road" title, the residents of Greenhill Lane had quietly agreed amongst themselves that it was better to give Loopy Lilly a wide berth. This approach usually worked well, except on the odd occasion when the old woman would shuffle to the end of her drive and bark the strangest things to passers-by.

"What year do you think it is?" and "Why does my face look like this?" were probably the most common and awkward questions she would spring on people. Most of the Greenhill Lane residents would smile kindly and continue on their way, leaving Loopy Lilly to amuse herself.

At the other end of the street, and unaware of Loopy

Lilly, eleven-year-old Lucas Ambrose of 121 Greenhill Lane had moved in with his mom, dad and little sister Sarah just a year ago. Lucas had tried his best to settle in at his new school. Moving house and starting high school had been a daunting challenge but he was making steady progress, Lucas was finally beginning to navigate the new school's various blocks and scramble his way through the crowds of bigger students. Sarah Ambrose, on the other hand, had no trouble fitting in with her peers. Her golden ringlets and chocolate eyes, that melted when she smiled, seemed to draw everyone in and stick them to her like honey. Lucas was a stark contrast to his sister. After a recent growth spurt, he had become long and gangly. His hair, though a similar shade of blonde to his sister, seemed to grow out in awkward tufts like a scarecrow.

Even in his early years Lucas had been socially awkward. At the age of five, in an effort to help their son come out of his shell, his parents had brought him a dog. Lucas had named his black and grey spaniel "Davey Jones". He'd enjoyed taking Davey Jones out for walks and his parents started to breathe a sigh of relief, hopeful that their shy son was coming out of his shell at last. They had just brought the puppy a shiny name tag when Davey Jones had unexpectedly fallen ill and died, leaving Lucas quietly devastated. He had refused to speak at all for two weeks after that. The arrival of his little sister a few years later had convinced his parents that their odd little Lucas would have a lifelong best friend.

In a sense they had been right, Sarah had provided her older brother with a welcome cover in social situations. Lucas had developed a knack for steering clear of people and often, when in public, he would simply melt into the background behind his sister, happily allowing her to take the spotlight. When Sarah wasn't around, he would retreat inside himself entirely, avoiding people wherever possible.

Lucas had found this last year particularly challenging. Even after leaving Sarah behind for high school, Lucas discovered she was still more popular than him. Many of his peers knew his sister outside of school and had labelled him "Sarah Ambrose's weird brother" and so he'd found it difficult to make friends. It had been hard work navigating this new and unfamiliar territory; however, this week had been different! This week he'd actually managed a short conversation or two with a few of his classmates. So, at 3:20 p.m. when he cycled home that day, Lucas pored over his brief, but positive interactions with a visible grin.

"Life is good. I'm making friends and I've got ages till my 6 p.m. curfew" he smiled to himself.

He was only mildly aware of his surroundings as they whipped past his bike, and was far more interested in analysing the new sensation in his stomach that was not altogether unpleasant. Completely lost in his thoughts, Lucas didn't see Loopy Lilly as she shuffled directly into his path.

"Wooooah!" he yelped as his bike brakes squealed indignantly, bringing him almost nose to wrinkly nose with his elderly neighbour. The boy barely had time to catch his breath when his creepy neighbour thrust out a bony hand and clasped his shoulder.

"Do you know me?" she croaked, "Please, have you seen my parents? They're looking for me!"

The young boy's body quivered in the old lady's grasp. He pulled his shoulder instinctively from her cold hand as his foot pawed blindly at the bike pedal, desperate to get away. The shock of actually hearing the old witch speak directly to him was scary enough, but now his unsuccessful escape attempt had sent Lucas's heart racing. His delay meant that he was unable to avoid her bizarre questioning.

"P-parents?" He had no idea what to say next and the rest of his words were suffocated as his throat tightened in fear. His voice had left him, but the boy's mind still raced.

This woman had to be in her 70s, he thought to himself *If her parents were alive, they'd probably be nearly a hundred years old by now*!

He wrestled with these numbers and, as he did, the elderly lady locked eyes with him. He noticed with surprise that Loopy Lilly's eyes were a brilliant cobalt blue, and he recognised the shade immediately. His mom had come home one day carrying tins of paint and announced that she couldn't stand their boring cream bathroom one second longer.

"I want this room to be a refuge of rest and relaxation," she had declared with a smile and, swinging two large paint tins with 'cobalt blue' printed on them and she set out to achieve exactly that. Lucas had loved this particular shade of blue. Whenever he used the bathroom, it made him feel as though he was being gently wrapped in a tranquil sea. Loopy Lilly's deep blue stare had disarmed him briefly, and he felt like he was back home.

The blue eyes blinked, interrupting his thoughts.

"I'm sorry...I think I'm lost" she whimpered "I went out a little while ago and I-I lost track of time, you see?" The old lady's voice sounded timid and small, and her bottom lip trembled slightly. "I tried to get my time back, of course, back down the alley and right...or was it left?" she mumbled, now more to herself than Lucas.

"Wrong way. Stay away..." Loopy Lilly trailed off into an incoherent babble and released her grip on the boy's shoulder.

He watched, frozen, as the old lady ambled her way back inside her house, slamming the door behind her and leaving the young boy shaking from head to toe.

Minutes passed while Lucas contemplated the strange lady and her blue eyes. The same blue that made him think of home, seemed so eerily misplaced on the face of Loopy Lilly. His eyes dropped to his wristwatch. Since the house move, he and his sister had both been allowed to make their own way to and from school and occasionally to the shops or the library. However, their parents had coupled this new freedom with a very strict curfew.

"Home by no later than 6 p.m. and don't talk to strangers," his dad would say as he waved them off.

Now his father's warning echoed through his head. Snapping him out of his stupor, he glanced at the batman watch on his wrist—5:56 p.m. How was that even possible? He could swear a whole half hour had just evaporated during his creepy encounter with Loopy Lilly. He threw his leg over his bike and peddled hard.

5:57 p.m. He was going to be in big trouble, and he still had over half the road to get round! Greenhill Lane's sinister looking alleyway loomed towards him and beckoned. In a very uncharacteristic moment, he decided to take the short cut. Turning hard he weaved down the slender passage, hitting the uneven paving stones with a violent crunch! His bones rattled as the bike clattered and flew down the narrow path. The ground beneath him sloped steeply downward and he gathered even more speed. The surrounding grey walls that marked the edges of people's gardens began to blur.

Suddenly the front wheel of his bike hit something. It may have been an uneven paving slab or a tree root but at the speed Lucas was going it was impossible to tell. The front wheel buckled, and the bike frame jerked forwards, sending its rider flying over the handlebars and sprawling onto the hard ground. Dazed and aching, his head was swimming with Loopy Lilly's warning; "The alleyway...stay away," she had said.

"Stupid old woman," he grumbled defiantly. "She *should* have told me to watch for the death-trap hill down here."

He sat up and assessed the damage. His trousers were ripped, and his knees were skinned and sore. He checked his watch; it was cracked, and the second hand had stopped moving altogether. Lucas groaned when he noticed the front wheel of his bike was lodged in between the thick roots of a tree. The wheel spokes had sprung out haphazardly, piercing his tyre like knitting needles.

He pulled himself to his feet and tried to tug the broken bike out of the tree, but it was hopeless. The wheels were jammed tightly somehow in between those python-sized tree roots. The boy heaved and twisted the metal frame as hard as he could, and his punctured tyres hissed in protest, but the bike wouldn't budge. Frustrated and defeated, he kicked the closest tree root and stubbed his toe. After yelling a few choice swear words, Lucas stood up straight and waited for the throbbing in his toe to subside.

He looked back at the steep hill he'd just flown down on

his bike and let out a low whistle. Daylight from above fought its way down the tall walls of the passage, illuminating the jagged and dangerous path he'd just descended. At the bottom of the slope, he noticed a nest of broken cement and cracked slabs with razor sharp edges that, thankfully, had not caused him more serious damage. Worse still, just a few inches from where he'd landed, the ground sparkled with dozens of tiny shards of broken glass. He heaved himself shakily to his feet. His head hurt but his breathing steadied as he took a look around.

The oppressive walls on either side were splattered with indecipherable graffiti, sporting names he didn't recognise. Some names appeared more than once, and every few feet was punctuated with the word 'HELP' written in countless different ways in pen, paint and sometimes even etched directly into the brick. His eyes scanned the rest of the wall's surface, hopeful for some light-hearted insults, comical drawings perhaps, or rude suggestions more typical of a suburban alley. Anything to detract from the growing collection of disturbing pleas for help.

His gaze landed on a large, floral-patterned 'L' that looked as though it must have taken some time and a little artistic flare. This single letter had a bold, dark outline and had been filled in with many intricate swirls and patterns. The letter had been so detailed that he hadn't noticed it was actually followed by the rest of a name; Lilly.

His examination of the wall's graffiti was interrupted by the unexpected sound of a dog barking. The noise had sounded far away, but a moment later the lost boy jumped out of his skin when he felt something brush his leg accompanied by the patter of paws. He hadn't noticed a dog anywhere nearby and an impossible layer of mist now seemed to have materialised out of nowhere, masking everything below his knees. The boy felt ice cold beads of sweat trickling down the back of his neck. Lucas began to panic.

Where had the sudden fog come from? What had brushed past him and what was that panting sound?

It drew close to him then moved away again. Amidst the landslide of increasing worries, he felt something skim his ankle and he cried out and leapt forward, landing with a soft squelch.

"HELP ME PLEASE!" the desperate boy hollered at the top of his lungs.

His voice echoed and bounced back at him mockingly. His head swivelled from one tall wall to the other, surely one of the neighbouring houses would have heard him? Lucas's ears were ringing as echoes bounced back and forth surrounding him in a din. He could feel fresh tears sting his eyes.

"HEEEEEEEEEEEEEEELP!" he screamed again, this time for as long and loud as he could manage until his throat burned.

There was no reply. No sound of people scurrying to his aid. His eyes raked the top of the tall walls, but no nosey neighbours poked their heads over to see what all the fuss was. His only company was the unnatural fog and that relentless panting. As it drew closer it sounded wet and eager. The terrified boy dragged his reluctant legs forward. The ground beneath the fog started to feel loose and swampy. Each time he lifted one of his feet above the blanket of fog, it became heavier and increasingly caked in mud. After just a few steps, he couldn't pull his left foot up anymore. He howled and jolted violently as the lower half of his leg was seized and sucked deep into the mud beneath him. The wet ground was going to swallow him.

"Help!" Lucas whimpered, a suffocating wave of hopelessness pushed him further down. The quiet suburban road he had left just a short time ago felt miles away in another world. A much brighter world. This monstrous corridor was going to gobble him up and he could do nothing but sob quietly, alone.

His cheeks felt wet, at first with tears that streamed down his face then a different kind of wet, strange but a little familiar. A damp, leathery nose pressed itself against his face and a soft grey ear tickled him. Instinctively he reached out and stroked the friendly dog that now had its whole face in his, earning a big wet lick in return. Wiping his eyes, Lucas watched the dog wag its tail and paw at him gently. The dog seemed friendly and was, perhaps, a neighbour's dog he'd already met and forgotten about. Too tired to question the animal's timely appearance and feeling emboldened, now that he was no longer totally alone, the broken and battered boy rallied himself and clawed at the mud around his foot. The dog helped too, pawing gently at the soggy earth that held the boy until at last, Lucas was able to pull himself free, landing in a messy heap on the floor.

"Thank you," he wheezed, stroking the dog's mucky face as it wagged its tail and barked happily. Lucas lay on his back, waiting to catch his breath.

He took a good look at the dog, and he could have sworn it was his Davey Jones, just a little bigger! While still breathing heavily he seized the small brass tag that dangled around the dog's neck and held it still to read; "Davey Jones!"

"Wha-what? Davey, but..." his head was thumping from the effort of pulling himself free.

Davey Jones! The letters on the little brass tag taunted him. How could this be the same dog that had died just as he had begun to love it? Lucas shook his head fiercely in an attempt to shake out such impossible notions. This place was doing something to him, messing with his mind. He'd already been gone too long. If he didn't get back soon his parents would have people scouring the area for him. He tried not to think of how embarrassed he would be in school once everyone heard about him getting so lost down an alley that he needed a rescue party, his less than stellar reputation was about to take an epic nosedive. The dog looked up at him expectantly.

"Come on, boy," he crooned.

Having the dog with him was a great comfort. He had begun to understand that this passage was a highly unnatural place with its own rules. It was futile to try and understand why Davey Jones had come back to him. The two of them pushed on together. While the ground beneath them remained mercifully solid, the high walls had not shrunk an inch so all they could do was to continue trudging on. The dog pranced ahead, much happier on the firm surface, providing a cheerful distraction from their surroundings. As they marched the boy breathed heavily and his head ached.

"How long was this damn path anyway?" he exclaimed, having no idea how much time had passed. Neither Davey Jones nor the path had a reply.

Lucas caught himself wishing he'd gone back the way he came. Although the route had been hell, at least he knew that the way behind him had a definite end that led back to the world. The probably-wasn't-Davey-Jones dog continued to lead the way, spurring them both on, but Lucas was in pain and unable to keep up with him. Every muscle was burning, and his joints ached in a way they never had before. He began to feel as though the nuts and bolts that held his body together were slowly rusting. The lost boy's hands and face, though almost free of mud, felt swollen and leathery. He couldn't wait to get home and take a nice long shower.

He began to feel a steady burning in his chest and lungs, so he paused, leaning against a lamppost to catch his breath. What a day! The dog looked up at him and even Davey Jones was beginning to look tired. His tail had ceased wagging and drooped to the ground.

"I'm gonna sleep for a week when I get home, Davey," Lucas told him. His voice sounded oddly cracked and strained. "Have a nice long bath and you know what, boy? I'm not ever coming down this damn shortcut again," he laughed.

The forced laughter bounced off the high walls sounding hollow and cold as it echoed down the passage. Once the noise had dissipated, he took a moment, and his eyes studied the lamppost he was leaning on. It wore a crudely made sign and a tired yellow poster. The sign, which pointed in the direction he was headed, read 'Greenhill Lane'. He heaved a sigh of relief and then his eyes travelled to the laminated poster that had been zip tied to the lamppost a little lower down.

It was a missing persons poster for a young girl. He'd seen things like this on the television but never in real life. The picture looked weathered and was dated nearly a year ago, the bottom was now completely illegible. This girl had a pretty smile and curly hair. At the top, in bold, was her name and a simple sentence; 'Lilly Langer. Missing from her loving home on Greenhill Lane'. She looked to be around Lucas's age and, though faded, the photo of the girl was still visible. Her face was unfamiliar, but Lucas recognised the eyes. Those bright cobalt-blue eyes were unforgettable as they seemed to look right through him!

"Loopy Lilly," Lucas whispered.

He couldn't explain it, but the face in the photo had the same eyes and cheekbones. It was the much younger face of the same creepy lady that had accosted him just an hour or so ago, asking after her parents and warning him not to come down this alleyway.

He had been rooted to the spot while he examined the impossible photo, and he began to feel as though the mud that coated him from head to toe was starting to dry and turn solid. Every movement seemed to take a tremendous amount of effort. Lucas willed his aching limbs forward, groaning in a laboured tone that didn't sound like him. Just beyond the lamppost, a well-groomed hedge led the way to sunlight and the bright world outside of this awful corridor. He clasped one hand around Davey-jones collar who seemed to be moving much slower too. In his free hand, he snatched at handfuls of green hedges. Harsh sunlight made his eyes so bleary that the dog at his side appeared older and greyer. He reached to pet him and froze, his own hand appeared wrinkled, and his skin was leathery. His batman watch looked the same, but it sagged and rattled around his thin wrists and curiously, the second hand had started ticking again.

Lucas touched his face and traced along deep crevices and wrinkles that had never been there before. His legs trembled and he staggered into a puddle. As the ripples of the puddle subsided around his soaking wet feet, he gazed horrified at his reflection. An elderly man stared back at him. He moved when Lucas moved, and cried the very instant Lucas began to cry until both Lucas and his new reflection fell to their knees.

"Davey?" he croaked in a haggard tone, but his faithful dog was nowhere to be seen.

"Hey, old boy," a friendly voice called. "You ok there, pal?"

He watched as a young man cautiously approached him. The man seemed to be in his twenties and looked athletic. He smiled kindly at Lucas but also looked wary of him.

"Can I call someone for you, buddy? What's your name?" he asked, slowly removing a phone from his shorts pocket.

"I-my, my dog," Lucas croaked. "I'm Lucas Ambrose."

"Ambrose. Ambrose, where have I heard..." the man paused and shallow wrinkles creased his forehead briefly, then his face lit up "Ambrose! That family left a long time ago, before my family moved here. I heard about them from my neighbour. Apparently, their son went missing one day. They looked for him for months, of course, but when no one found nothing I guess they couldn't face living here anymore. Was all quite a drama, my neighbour says." The guy's expression shifted to a respectful somber "All very sad, think he was only young."

"What?" Lucas cried. Hot, fresh tears found their way through the new wrinkles that spanned his face "How? How long was I gone?"

The young man looked completely taken aback but smiled awkwardly. "Hey, chap, easy there, we'll get you where you need to be. Are you from the retirement home on Bethany Street?"

Lucas was too distraught to reply. The kindly stranger smiled and began making some calls. He could barely breathe or think. He didn't even notice a woman approach him until she placed a warm gentle hand on his shoulder. He looked round to see the familiar face of Loopy Lilly Langer. It was oddly reassuring to see that she had not changed. Her face was the same as it had looked a few hours ago except now her wrinkles glistened with fresh tears.

"I got lost too," the old lady whispered, under the sound of the man chatting into his phone. "I cut down that way on the way home. I-I was 14 years old when I took the shortcut on Greenhill Lane."

She made a quiet whimpering sound, and her eyes flashed towards Lucas, that brilliant shade of cobalt blue. They looked so young and afraid.

Sniffing loudly, she continued, "Just last year I was a 14-year-old girl. I walked down the alley, and I saw- I saw missing posters with my face on and I'd only been gone a short time. I was lost down there, and I don't know what happened. I came out of that path all old like a granny."

Lilly Langer wrinkled up her nose and gazed at her hands as though looking at them for the first time. "No one believed me. I tried to tell them I got lost and when I asked about my family, people told me they were all long gone. Time was broken, it felt like I was lost for hours but for everyone else I was gone for years. When I was leaving that place, it made me old just like it did to you but that wasn't all, I've never got any older since then, ever! It's like someone hit a fast forward button on my age and then the pause button.

"Time is always going to be different for us now, it's scary and confusing. Everyone thinks you went missing years ago, but I remember telling you to stay away from that alley like it was yesterday."

Lucas gritted his teeth to keep from throwing up "No!" he gnashed. His head was pounding. "That's impossible. I wasn't gone long; it was just a stupid shortcut." His voice wheezed, "I can't be old. Things like that can't happen in the real world. Time can't break!" even as he said it out loud his body contradicted him, leaving him breathless.

Lilly's words crawled through his brain. The way she spoke pierced his heart, she sounded so timid and scared. He knew it was all true, the alley wasn't only a brutal passage, it was a wound in time. Both of them had gotten lost in that place and time itself had abandoned them. Just in that moment, Lucas caught sight of a girl he'd known from school walking down the opposite side of the road. She looked taller and had white ear buds in and seemed to be singing along to the music, oblivious to the old man staring at her. Lucas lifted his hand an inch and then paused. What could he say? An old man claiming to be the quiet boy from school was going to scare her and make him sound crazy. He watched, feeling hollow as she carried on her way singing and smiling, her whole life still before her. He wondered if they might have become friends.

When he finally tore himself away Lucas saw Lilly brushing away her own tears, "People always talked about the shortcut on Greenhill Lane," Lilly croaked in a husky tone. "I remember the teachers and other kids at school saying that people go missing down there sometimes. I thought it was just a silly story, everybody did. It's all true. It's a forgetting place, where you forget where you are, then everyone else forgets you, then time forgets you too." Lilly's voice was almost a whisper,

"I don't think that it's part of our world".

The Gallows Grave

By Richard Tyndall, from his book 'The Aldwark Tales'

Some two miles southwest of Aldwark, along the old straight road that splits the county in two, lies the village of Fernbank. Dating back to Saxon or perhaps even Roman times, these days the village has expanded far beyond its original boundaries to fill a broad strip of land on the ridge between the road and the river flood plain. The village has lost much of its character as a result of the expansion and is now little different to hundreds of similar settlements across the shires which have fallen victim to ever growing populations of newcomers with scant knowledge of country ways and country life.

There were other ways in which Fernbank resembled other communities across England. For there was a man – a poor description but it will have to suffice for the purposes of this narrative – a man who went by the name of Bobby Grayling. There is a Bobby Grayling in every parish in England. They may not look the same, may bear no external resemblance to each other whatsoever, but in nature, mannerisms and downright crookedness all these men – for they are invariably male – are brothers in everything but name. Normally there is never more than one of these malignant creatures in each village; no community being able to survive with more than a single such drain on its physical and mental wellbeing. In Fernbank, Bobby Grayling was the sickness that sapped the strength of the community.

Grayling did not work. At least he undertook no sort of paid employment like his neighbours. He had decided very early in life that work was - to quote him when he was being less than circumspect - 'a mug's game'. So these days Grayling was 'unfit' for work as a result of a minor accident many years earlier, which had caused such irreparable damage to his back as to make it impossible for him to hold down a job. Or that was what he claimed and, as is the manner in this day and age, his claims were certified by a doctor too busy to pay real attention and more concerned for people with real injuries and illnesses than for one man who just wanted to get one over on the system. And so his career-ending injuries were accepted without question by the authorities, certified with a note in a file and set in stone forever more.

Of course, suggestions were made for light forms of work away from the factory floor, but he could easily deflect such suggestions with a few carefully placed medical conditions. Manual work was right out as his back would never take the strain. The same applied to any office work that required him to sit for any great length of time as that made his back go into spasm. Walking was agreeable but not when carrying anything. He ensured that, whilst making heartfelt declarations of his wish to earn his keep, he was seen as such a burden to any prospective employer that he was assured of never finding a real job.

In the end the authorities admitted defeat – though in truth they had never really tried very hard to avoid the decision. Bobby was signed off on permanent sick leave and received a generous payment from his former employers and a healthy pension from the state. And all before he had even completed his fourth decade of life.

After a year or so of doing nothing much and generally enjoying life, Grayling found that the money from his employer was starting to run low and the pension, generous as it was, was nowhere near enough to keep him and his family in the manner to which they would like to become accustomed. As a result, he looked around for something he could do that would provide a little bit of money on the side but would not involve anything too strenuous. By chance a cousin had recently acquired a metal detector which, considering the force at which it must have hit the ground when it fell off the back of the lorry, was in remarkably good condition. A touch of gentle persuasion, combined with the payment of a small fee, ensured that the instrument was quickly acquired by Grayling and he embarked on his new career as a treasure hunter.

Grayling now became a particularly low form of pond life in the deep, wide pool that is archaeology. He was driven by one thing and one thing alone; the prospect of finding something valuable enough that he might make a few pounds or, even better, a few thousand pounds from a sale to a private 'collector'. It was theft in everything but name and, as such, was immensely attractive.

So, over the next few years, this man whose injuries prevented him undertaking any form of manual labour was to be seen in fields all over the parish and beyond digging away in search of buried treasure. This poor invalid who could carry nothing more than a cup of tea was to be seen on a warm summer's evening striding proudly across the fields bearing a weighty pack filled to the brim with pot, stone and metal to be examined later in the safety of his home. This cripple who could not sit for more than a few minutes without his back going into painful spasm could be found, hour after hour, at his desk poring over some tiny scrap of bronze buckle or a medieval coin; cleaning and preparing to ensure he got the very best of prices from the select group of collectors who he hoped to tempt into discrete visits to his home to purchase the rare and beautiful items he had found in the fields around Aldwark.

Nor was Grayling restricted to simply combing the open fields in the hope of a chance discovery. Early in his newfound career he had realised that if he really wanted to make some money, he needed to be searching in those places known to have been of importance centuries earlier; the prehistoric burial mounds, Roman villas and forts, Saxon cemeteries and deserted medieval villages. These were the places that would yield the best rewards for the least work. These were the places that Bobby and his metal detector needed to visit. Unfortunately for Grayling, such sites are of value to more than just treasure hunters. Centuries of neglect and treasure hunting by gentleman antiquarians had led government to pass laws protecting these places from the worst ravages of greed and well-meant but incompetent archaeological research. Designated as historic monuments, most of the really interesting sites were now legally out of bounds to Grayling and his faithful detector.

Not, of course, that he intended to let that stop him for a minute. It just meant he had to carry out more of his detecting under the cover of darkness or poor weather. Fog was a positive blessing. It may have made his task a little less enjoyable at times but if he was lucky the rewards might compensate for any temporary discomfort. And so it was that Bobby Grayling became that most disreputable of practitioners in an already tarnished hobby: A Nighthawk.

It heartens the author to report that, in his new vocation, Bobby Grayling was a notable failure. Assisted by his cousin Ronny - a congenital idiot whose opposing thumb and upright stance mistakenly led people to assume the presence of some form of human intelligence - in a less than a year he was able to strip the parish of Fernbank of anything resembling archaeological heritage. To an archaeologist what he found was almost priceless, but to Bobby it was little better than garbage; bits of pot, bones and the occasional coin. The sort of thing that might sell for a few pounds but would never be enough to make a living out of.

Still, he was nothing if not persistent. Once Fernbank had been pillaged, it was a natural step to move further afield and start the scouring of adjacent parishes up and down the old Roman road. There were sites aplenty for anyone with the right tools and sufficient lack of moral rectitude, but a trove of any real value always managed to elude the nighthawk. Crime, it seemed, just would not pay. And so, as time went by and Bobby failed to dig up his fortune, his thoughts began to turn to the one site he had always sworn he would never touch.

It was a site that had particularly fascinated and haunted Grayling for many a year, even before he had discovered his true vocation as a grave robber. As a boy he had been afraid of little in the village. He was, after all, a consummate bully and sneak, and had always maintained a coterie of associates – I hesitate to call them friends – willing to watch his back, for a suitable price of course. But there had been one thing that 'associates' could not protect him from, one fear that had been with him for as long as he could remember, and that was undiminished by time or adulthood. A place that both attracted and repelled him in equal measure and which lay close by in the adjacent parish of Stoches.

Upon leaving the southwestern fringes of Fernbank, the old straight road crosses an area of low marshy land close by the river. The location makes the river side meadows prone to regular flooding during the months of autumn and winter, and waters regularly lap against the raised bank of the road which acts in the manner of a dyke, protecting the fields and villages behind from the worst of the winter inundation. Only on the rarest of occasions in the most severe of seasons have the waters overwhelmed the road to bring misery to the hamlets beyond. On the far side of the marshes the road passes through the ancient village of Stoches, which sits upon a sandy ridge close by the site of the Roman fort of Pontus Niger. Unlike its neighbouring village, Stoches has escaped the worst of the development that has afflicted the rest of the district and, even today, remains a compact settlement with all the benefits of a shire hamlet.

This quiet village, disturbed only by the incessant growl of traffic negotiating the curves and bends that curl past the local pub, enters our story as the home of one of Grayling's uncles, now long dead but pertinent to the tale, as it was to his house that young Bobby was forced to walk every Friday evening, while his parents drank themselves into oblivion at Fernbank's riverside inn. The house and the uncle were both unremarkable. Actually, that is unfair to the man, who was the one good thing in Grayling's wretched life, and who did all in his power to deflect the boy from his inevitable slide into indolence and crime. But for the sake of this tale, further description of either the uncle or his residence are unnecessary.

What is of note for our story is the field to the south of the road just as it rose up onto the bank and entered the village. For in this field was a mound, some fifty feet in diameter and perhaps ten feet in height above the rest of the pasture. Known locally as the Gallows Grave, it was this mound and the field it occupied that formed the focus for all Bobby Grayling's greatest fears and nightmares. Every Friday night he would make the mile and a half walk from Fernbank, down the footpath to meet the road at the edge of the marshes and then along the verge, across the low ground until he came in sight of the ridge and the first lights of the houses of Stoches village. In the middle of the year this could be a pleasant enough walk. In the days of his youth there were few cars on the road and none of the great lorries which now made walking the route so hazardous.

On a warm summer's evening the prospect of an evening with his uncle, perhaps some fishing on the river below the old hall or a wander through the woods behind the water meadows, was enough to suck him across the marshes in a mood of excited anticipation. But as the year drew to a close and the evenings grew dark before he had even finished his lessons, he came to loathe that walk along the old Roman road. With few cars and no streetlights, the trip became a stumble through the darkness struggling to avoid the potholes and pitfalls in the roadside. As often as not, winds whipped off the open fields to the north across the river, driving rain, sleet or snow with them. However much he might plead, whatever the weather and however unwell he might be, Grayling's parents always insisted that he make that walk across the marshes to his uncle's house while they adjourned to the fireside at the inn.

Truth be told, Bobby could cope with the darkness, the weather and the cold. They were annoyances to be endured but would do little lasting harm, and there was always the prospect of hot toast and Ovaltine once he reached the warmth of his uncle's house. But before he reached that haven, there was one hurdle that had to be overcome, one terror that had to be faced every Friday evening, alone and in the dark.

Bobby Grayling had to walk past the field containing the Gallows Grave.

If you had asked him why that particular feature in that particular field should evoke such terror, young Grayling could probably have cited little more than deep-seated but apparently unfounded feelings of unease and repeated the common local legends about the place. It undoubtedly possessed a dark and unsettling history, having for many years been the site of a gallows upon which highwaymen and other 'ne'er do wells' were hung after a short and usually biased trial at the local hall. In the 18th century the 4th Earl of Stoches, one John Lovell, had earned the appellation of 'Gibbet John' as a result of the number of men he had successfully prosecuted for robbery, assault or just plain indolence on the Aldwark turnpike. All had ended their days hanging from the beam on Gallows Grave, in the process providing the mound with both its name and its bloody reputation.

Gibbet John himself had disappeared in mysterious circumstances in that very field one foggy winter's night in 1784 and no trace of his body had ever been discovered. After his death the mound had been used as the site for a post mill, taking advantage of the bitter winds that swept up onto the ridge from the marshes. But it was reputed an accursed place and after only a few years the mill was lost in a fire, the miller escaping with his life but nothing more.

After that, the mound had been left well alone and even successive generations of farmers refused to plough across that part of the field, leaving it instead as a circle of pasture on which the livestock refused to feed. Grayling knew the stories well enough and also the rumours of strange noises that drifted out of the field on misty nights when, in spite of the lack of wind, a creaking could be heard coming from the direction of the mound, like a wooden beam straining under the weight of a swinging corpse.

And so, every Friday evening Bobby Grayling would approach the bottom of the rise in darkness, stealing himself for a mad rush up the hill, past the field and into the village, not stopping or looking back until he reached the safety of his uncle's door.

Grayling had never forgotten those fearful winter walks. Even now, more than thirty years later, the thought of the Gallows Grave was still enough to produce dark moods and darker dreams. For this reason, the parish of

Stoches had remained mercilessly free of the ravages of metal detectors. Within the parish boundaries were many protected sites including the Roman fort, the medieval remains of what had once, before the terrible plagues of the 14th century, been a far more substantial village and even a battlefield where the King of England once put his rebellious subjects to the sword by the thousand. In spite of all of this, Grayling had steered well clear of Stoches and its blood-soaked mound.

Yet there was something about that field and the mound it contained that held an almost hypnotic sway over the nighthawk. Part of it was a need to confront his fears, a need to lay to rest the ghosts that had haunted him since childhood. But more than that, much more than that, was greed; the one underlying emotion that had driven him for so many years. The thought that the mound might contain something of great value; that it would finally provide that one priceless hoard of treasure that would see Grayling set for life. And yet his fear still held him back, still gripped his heart and persuaded him against exploration of the Gallows Grave. Then, finally, he found the one piece of information that tipped the balance and allowed his greed to overwhelm his fears.

The impetus came when Grayling gained access to the Sites and Monuments register. Here he found maps, dozens of wonderful, detailed maps which recorded every find, every earthwork and site of archaeological note in the county. The copies he had made of these maps had led him to every site that he had missed in the area although, as with all his previous excursions, he singularly failed to find anything of any great monetary value. But when he came to study the map which included the parish of Stoches he saw, for the first time, that the benighted mound on the edge of the village was far more than just the base of an old gallows or the footings for a mill. According to the notes on the maps, the Gallows Grave was nothing less than a Neolithic round barrow, the burial mound of some prehistoric noble who would undoubtedly, as far as Grayling was concerned, have been buried with great ceremony and even greater treasure. When he saw that note all his fears were forgotten and he determined that, as soon as possible, he would take his detector and search the mound for the treasure he knew would rightfully soon be his.

So it was that, on one cold, clear November night, Bobby Grayling and his semi-moronic cousin Ronny set out from Fernbank to walk the path out to the old road. From there they cut across into the fields to avoid being spotted by travellers in their vehicles. It was a clear night and finding their way through the hedges proved little obstacle to their progress so that, within the hour and with the clock standing at just before one in the morning, that found themselves stood on the edge of the field looking across at the Gallows Grave. The field was ploughed, tilled and planted with winter wheat which appeared as a green fur some four inches in height, coating the dark soil beneath. There was a fine sheen of frost across the whole field and there, barely visible on the far side was the grass covered mound of Gallows Grave.

Early in his life Bobby had decided he needed a nickname, something that set him out as an individual, a man apart from those poor saps who spent their days in toil and their nights in fitful sleep. After much thought he had settled upon the name Otter. An otter was a sleek, quick-witted animal, handsome, elusive, a hunter; all the things that Bobby imagined to be part of his character. Of course, simply deciding you wanted a nickname was not enough. You had to convince people to use it as well. This was all the more difficult when, as in Bobby's case, those who knew him saw him as more of a toad than an otter.

As it turned out, the only person who could be persuaded to use the nickname was Ronny and that was only after he had been bribed with large quantities of Dolly Mixtures. If one could forget his extreme idiocy for a moment, then these sweets were Ronny's one great weakness and Grayling always ensured he had a twist or three in his pocket to guarantee his cousin's unquestioning obedience. It was times like this, stood on the edge of a frosted field in the small hours of the morning looking over at a reputedly haunted burial mound, that Grayling was thankful for the lack of imagination in his moronic relation. Give Ronny enough sweets and his brain melted in the sugar rush so that he would obey the most ludicrous of instructions without the slightest hesitation – well, no more than was normal for him anyway.

"Wah we doin', Otter?" Ronny asked through a mouth full of half chewed fondant.

"What we are doing, dear cousin, is making ourselves rich."

As he replied, Grayling never took his eyes off the mound that lay shrouded in darkness on the extreme limits of his vision. Even on a night like this, with the constellations clear in the sky and the Milky Way a soft white blur across the heavens, the Gallows Grave seemed to generate its own deep shadow in which it lurked menacingly.

"Pick up the bags and follow me, Ronny. We're going to do a bit of digging."

They set forth across the field towards the mound, watching all the while for signs of movement on the road or lights in the houses a few dozen yards away on the edge of the village. More than once in his short career as a nighthawk, Grayling had been forced to flee after falling foul of a nosy neighbour or an observant police patrol. They had never caught him yet but Bobby had learned that, even in the most unlikely of circumstances, he should always keep half an eye on the lookout for the authorities.

Grayling spent the next hour sweeping the field close to the barrow, listening intently for the squeaks and whines in his earphones that would indicate the presence of metal. A good nighthawk could even tell what sort of metal he was detecting, by the tone of the feedback from the detector and the flick of the needle on the dial set into the handle of the machine. And although he had only been detecting a few years, Grayling was very, very good. This night he knew what he was after, and it wasn't iron.

Most of the time, iron turned out to be horseshoe nails or bits of old farm machinery, rusted slices of ploughshare and twisted pieces of threshing machine. This night particularly, Bobby wasn't going to waste time on those. He was here for treasure and that meant gold, silver or bronze. Although the grave itself dated from the late Neolithic and so, in spite of Grayling's daydreams, was unlikely to contain anything of real value as far as treasure was concerned, Grayling knew from his books that later peoples, particularly in the Bronze Age and much later in the Saxon period, had held these mounds in great veneration and had often reused them for burying their own dead. If he was lucky here was every chance of finding Bronze Age weapons or a Saxon hoard hastily buried to hide it from the approaching Danes.

But after an hour, with Grayling straining to pick up even the slightest trace of hidden metal, nothing of any value had been uncovered. He pulled the headphones from his ears for a moment and looked about him. Ronny sat on the lower slopes of the mound facing the road, watching for cars and clutching his spade in anticipation of digging to be done once Grayling indicated he had something worth investigating. He was cold, the frosted ground was damp through his trousers and, having finished his twist of dolly mixtures, he was feeling more than a little rebellious.

"What we doin', Otter?" he asked for the second time that night.

"I've already told you, Ronny. We are looking for treasure," Grayling snapped back.

"Have we found any yet?"

"Does it look like it, you idiot? Now shut up and let me think for a minute?"

Ronny looked at his cousin for a moment and then asked the obvious question. "Why haven't you looked on the mound, Otter? I would 'ave thought that the treasure would be buried in the mound. Don'cha think we should look in the mound?"

Grayling reflected that his cousin was right of course. The mound was the obvious place to look. He had convinced himself that by checking the area around the mound first he was just being thorough but he knew that, in truth, what he was really doing was just delaying the moment when he had to step upon that grassy knoll. If there was any treasure to be found it was upon that mound and there was no longer any reason for putting off his search of it.

He advanced to the edge of the plough soil close to where Ronny sat, and stood for a moment looking at the barrow. He told himself it was just a mound of earth. He knew that was all it was. A pile of soil covering the remains of a man that had been dead for four thousand years. But still... there was something. He remembered old Gibbet John who had disappeared somewhere in this field. He remembered the stories of the creaking beam and the fear he had felt as a child every time he had to walk past this place.

And then he looked down at Ronny. Simple Ronny, sat there on the mound without a care in the world - except perhaps that his toes might fall off if they stayed out in this field much longer. Happy Ronny, if you ignored the cold, hoping that Grayling might reach into his pocket and bring out another of those twists of dolly mixtures. Grayling laughed at his own stupid superstition and, reaching into his pocket to make Ronny happy, he stepped forward onto the grass.

The ground was softer than he had expected but, as he passed the sweets to his cousin and took another step up the slope, he concluded that this was just an illusion as a result of stepping off the hard, frozen soil of the field and onto the springy grass of the mound. He continued to climb the barrow.

It should have taken no more than eight or ten steps to reach the summit but, as he approached the crest, Grayling realised that he did not seem to be as high as he expected. The ground appeared to be very soft indeed, almost like he was walking through a patch of deep mud. He turned to look back at his cousin still sat at the base of the barrow and as he did, he heard the unmistakeable creak of an old wooden beam, straining under a heavy swinging load.

Bobby gasped and looked down at his feet. He was less than two yards from the top of the mound but now, as he regarded the ground, he realised that he had sunk up to his knees into the earth of the Gallows Grave. He tried to lift his leg, but the soil seemed to grip his ankle and prevented him from pulling his foot free. The sound of the beam creaking in the wind grew ever louder. Yet there was no wind.

Now Grayling was truly terrified, more frightened than he had ever been in his miserable life. He threw his detector down the slope towards his cousin and gave an anguished cry.

"Ronny!! Help, help me. I'm sinking, something's got my foot, Ronny, help me!"

For the first time, Ronny became aware that something was wrong. He jumped up from the mound and, stepping back onto the plough soil, looked up at his cousin sinking slowly into the top of the barrow.

"Wha... whatcha doin, Otter? What's happenin?"

"Help me, you idiot, something's got my foot. It's dragging me down, for Christ's sake, help meee..."

Ronny had already started up the mound towards his stricken cousin but as he heard Grayling's shouts and realised that this wasn't just a hole that his cousin had fallen into, that he had actually been seized by something beneath the ground, he stopped and started to back away down to the foot of the barrow. In the distance he could hear the creak of a tree bending in the wind and, though he had no idea what it might mean, he knew it frightened him. And he knew that there was no wind.

Grayling had now sunk up to his chest and the tight grip was moving inexorably up his body. The creaking had now risen in volume to the point where he could hardly hear his own voice as he cried out in desperation to his cousin, who was backing further and further away into the darkness, a look of terrified horror on his face.

"Ronny!! Ron..." the soil came up over his chin and flowed into his mouth, choking back the scream that tried to burst from Grayling's lips. Then it was over his nose, and he was being sucked down through the grass into the darkness of the Gallows Grave.

As Bobby's head finally disappeared beneath the ground and the creaking of the gallows faded away into the still silent November night, Ronny did the only think that any intelligent man would do. He turned and fled. He fled right out of the field, out of the village and out of the county. He was never seen again in the parish of Fernbank.

***

With the flight of Ronny, the fate of Bobby Grayling should have remained one of those mysteries never to be solved. His wife reported him missing but was generally unconcerned by his disappearance, assuming that he had probably 'done a runner' with a barmaid from one of the town centre pubs. It was certainly not unheard of and would be entirely in keeping with his character. Mrs Grayling had enough money in the bank to keep her happy and was sure that Bobby would turn up again sooner or later.

"Probably sooner, more's the pity."

But by strange chance it was less than a month before the mystery of what had become of the nighthawk was solved. And in the resolution of one mystery there invariably lie the seeds of many more. In this case those seeds soon sprouted into a whole forest of confusion.

It had been known for some time that the old Roman road was in need of improvement. The growth of Aldwark as a town and the need for people to travel into the city for work meant that there were simply too many vehicles on the road. So it was decided that a bright, big new road should be built parallel to, but some distance from, the original. As is traditional practice in these matters, even though it would still be some years before the building began, it was further decided that any archaeological features along the route should be investigated to ensure that nothing of any import would be destroyed by the wide strip of asphalt that would soon be sweeping northeast across the previously undisturbed farmland. Of course, given its prominence in the area, one of the first sites to be targeted by the archaeologists was the Gallows Grave. As it lay very close to the proposed route and there was every chance that it might be destroyed during the road building, it was decided that an excavation would be undertaken to ascertain if the local myths were true and there really was a tomb at the centre. That excavation started less than a fortnight after Bobby Grayling had disappeared on the barrow.

The excavators were dedicated and professional in their task. Everything was recorded, sectioned, drawn and photographed in meticulous detail. Every sherd of pottery was cleaned and studied for clues about its age. Every flake of flint was examined to identify those that had been worked. Soil was sieved, scraps of wood and leather were whisked away to the university for conservation, tiny animal bones, shells and husks of grain were all preserved for later analysis. And then, just over a week after they had begun digging, the archaeologists came upon the proof they had been looking for. As the soil and turf was stripped away from the top of the mound, a large cap stone, twice the size of a man, was revealed resting across the top of a stone lined chamber – a prehistoric tomb. Further excavation, again with photographs and drawings at every stage, revealed that the tomb consisted of three large upright megaliths capped with a fourth. Unusually perhaps, it was sealed as tight as could be, with every gap between the larger stones filled with smaller rocks and pieces of rubble to make an almost airtight chamber.

There was much debate over the next few days about the best way to remove the stones, and it was eventually decided to remove some of the smaller material, to allow a crane to be brought in, and a hawser passed through the chamber to secure the cap stone which could then be lifted out to reveal the insides of the tomb. This was duly accomplished and the whole team gathered around the stone chamber to witness the lifting of the capstone and to catch a glimpse of what was revealed within. It was a moment none of them would ever forget.

***

The police were, of course, involved. But an interview with Ronny, who was found hiding in a seedy guest house in Chester, left them just as bewildered as when they had first examined the scene. Specialist forensic experts were enlisted, the most eminent archaeologists were consulted. Every photograph, drawing and note was examined in minute detail. But at every turn the conclusions were the same. Prior to the removal of the huge capstone by the archaeology team, the tomb had remained undisturbed since the last days of the Neolithic some four thousand years before.

Once all the police investigations were completed, the coroner had to make some attempt to produce a verdict that would fit the extraordinary circumstances. There were simply so many questions left unanswered, so many impossibilities, that even the open verdict that was eventually passed down hardly seemed to do justice to the downright weirdness of the case.

The facts were simple enough. When the capstone was removed from the tomb, within there lay the remains of three people. The first, now reduced to a series of neatly stacked bones in one corner of the chamber in the tradition of his ancient culture, had been dead at least four thousand years. The second, also little more than bones in a shroud of rags and leather fittings, had apparently been a man of some importance judging by the rings on his fingers and the money in his pouch. These effects would later help his remains to be dated to the late 18th century, and a trawl of the records would allow the coroner to tentatively suggest the connection between this skeleton and the long-lost 4th Earl, Gibbet John.

The last man, his fingers bloody and torn where they had clawed at the stones, had been dead just under four weeks and otherwise bore not a mark of injury nor exhibited any sign of decomposition. Cause of death was determined as heart failure, but no autopsy could determine how long Grayling had lain in that unbroken, unending, impenetrable darkness before he finally succumbed to the terror. A broken penknife was found lying alongside the body and, as one of the diggers later observed, the underside of the capstone bore the scars of a desperate, futile attempt by the wretched man to scratch his way out through twenty-five tons of solid rock that had not been moved in more than four millennia.

What the coroner did not record in his verdict, and what would cause him many a sleepless night for the rest of his long life, was a short note inscribed amongst the papers of the 4th Earl, relating to the last man he condemned to the gallows before he himself disappeared from the world of men. He found the papers whilst trying to unearth some explanation, any explanation, for the mystery of the bodies in the Gallows Grave. What he found gave him little comfort.

"I curse these ignorant brutes who come before me daily. They serve no useful purpose and refuse to accept their station in life, their place in the natural order of things. Would that the ground itself might open up and swallow them, every last one of them and save me the trouble and expense of their trial.

"Any man who would stand against his rightful master, any low criminal who would kill and steal and lust and break God's commands deserves no better than to be sucked straight down into hell without so much as a stone to mark his passing.

"A curse on them all. Let the cold earth have them."

To B&B or not to B&B

By Kram Rednip

Henry Banff sat immobile behind the wheel of his Land Rover Discovery and waited.

A series of clangs, bangs and judderings from outside the enclosed car deck told him that the ferry had docked at last. A few of the other drivers sitting in cars in the files around him, waiting to disembark, had already started their engines.

'Don't know why they do that,' Henry mused to himself, wrinkling his nose. *'Be at least another twenty minutes before they open the doors and let us off.'*

The car deck smelt strongly of fish, mingled with the more familiar odours of grease and diesel oil. Henry wondered casually if Brittanny Ferries did a sideline transporting dead fish across the English Channel, on the off-days when they weren't transporting live passengers. He glanced at his watch: nearly 11.00 p.m. He felt quite tired, though he couldn't imagine why; after all, all he had done on the six-hour crossing was read dull consultant reports and drink strong French coffee. He sighed resignedly.

'Oh well, just have to be patient and wait, I suppose.'

Henry generally <u>was</u> a patient man, but he knew the immigration process following disembarkation would be tedious and so time-consuming now that Brexit had come to pass. He just wanted to get to his hotel and to bed.

He glanced at his smartphone, which he had laid down on the passenger seat beside him. Despite being in such enclosed surroundings there appeared to be a reasonably strong signal. He decided to call his wife.

"Hello, darling. What's that? Yes, I'm still on the ferry. We've just arrived in Caen, though, so shouldn't be too long now."

He frowned a little in concentration; the connection was not too good, and his wife's intonations sometimes made it tricky to understand exactly what she was saying. She was Ukrainian, and despite having lived in the UK for over 10 years had retained much of her Slavic accent.

"... yes, everything's fine, I'm just a little tired, Taniya, that's all. How are Patrick and Emily, in bed now I suppose? Give them my love tomorrow morning, they've both got a hard day at school, I know..."

After a little more domestic chit-chat he signed off to continue his wait in silence.

"Love you too, darling. Speak to you again tomorrow when I'm in Paris."

***

Henry was a Partner in the London offices of that celebrated international consulting firm the Arnaque

Partnership. In his late 50s now, he had been starting with some satisfaction to anticipate leaving the firm in a few years' time, perhaps to an idyllic early retirement in some picturesque, rural region of France – Normandy, for example. However, his vaguely self-indulgent musings in this regard had been somewhat jolted a few days before by a summons from the firm's managing partners in Paris to come over for an urgent meeting with them. Henry knew that 'urgent meetings' did not generally bring good news. And as the London Partner responsible for projects in Latin America and the Caribbean, two of his most recent projects (in Trinidad and Guyana respectively) had gone rather badly; in fact, both had been cancelled abruptly by the clients. Arnaque Managing Partners did not look kindly on their sources of revenue being curtailed in this manner. Henry therefore suspected that their summons to Paris might be to announce another curtailment – his own, in fact – thus bringing forward his comfortable retirement plans by a couple of years at least.

It was a bother, but Henry, who naturally had an easy-going and carefree disposition, was not really all that worried. *'After all,'* he said to himself, *'we're quite comfortably off; and I suppose they'd still give me some kind of severance package, in addition to my pension. And we won't need that much money anyway, not if we rent out the London house and buy that little place in Normandy or wherever we've been thinking of.'*

Henry was indeed very 'comfortably off' as he put it, it

was the ignominy of being fired he was more worried about. And ever the forward planner, he had extended his trip over to France by two days, specifically to have a look at some rather tempting properties his up-market estate agent had put him onto. This is why he had come over in his car, rather than simply taking the Eurostar direct to Paris.

***

More clanking and banging, and slowly the great metal doors to the car deck swung aside and open, revealing the bright arc-lights of the ferry terminal and the dark sky beyond. The files of cars started to move off and along the dock, towards the customs and immigration area a bit further along. Henry had not been wrong in his assumption that the immigration process would be slow and tedious. Sitting in his car in the queue, moving forward a couple of car lengths every few minutes, he consulted his watch again: now almost 11.30. It was a pity, he thought, that Taniya couldn't have come over with him. She would have enjoyed pottering around for a couple of days in the French countryside, inspecting the *manoirs* and *longeres* the estate agent had rustled up for them, thinking about how they might do them up, maybe in time go into the business of establishing a *gite rural* for British tourists... but of course, she couldn't come because of the children, who couldn't be taken out of school. Ah yes, the children; Henry realised, with a sudden pang of apprehension, that if he was indeed shafted by the managing partners and had to leave

Arnaque sooner than he had anticipated, the planned relocation to their rural French idyll would have to be put on ice. In a few years Patrick and Emily would be semi-independent, going to university probably, but right now it simply wouldn't be fair to remove them from the highly rated Clarendon School in Twickenham and dump them in some unremarkable *college* in some small French town miles from any major habitation. To his credit, Henry was fair-minded enough to clearly recognise this, and knew that Taniya would recognise it, too.

He had been married to Tatiania ('Taniya') for nearly 15 years now. They had initially met via an on-line dating site, that specialised in finding partners in the UK for Eastern European women (it was called 'Czech Mates').

Taniya was quite a few years younger than Henry, and like many Ukrainian women she was strikingly good-looking. Henry's colleagues at Arnaque, and many other friends and acquaintances, had cynically assumed the whole thing to be just a marriage of convenience; but in this, as with many other things concerning Henry and Taniya, they were entirely wrong. If Henry and Taniya didn't exactly love each other deeply, they both got something eminently worthwhile from their marriage, had stayed together and built a solid, equitable and infallibly even-tempered relationship that became more and more solid the longer it lasted. Many marriages, of convenience or otherwise, are not so fortunate in this respect.

'Of course, she's just a blonde bimbo who's seized her chance. Banff may not be a powerhouse of sexual dynamism, but he's quite blue-blooded, and he's worth a bob or two. Quite a decent catch, under the circumstances, for someone like her.'

Thus, the common trend of thinking regarding Mrs. Taniya Banff (nee Tatiana Ostapenko of Zhytomir, in central Ukraine). But here certainly, the common thinking was indeed entirely wrong. Taniya, though unquestionably blonde, was not a 'bimbo': in fact, she was highly sensitive, intelligent and educated, a qualified psychologist with a master's degree from Taras Shevchenko University in Kyiv. She had married Henry – who in so far as these things can be measured, was far less intelligent than she was – simply because she liked him the first time they met, and because during subsequent meetings he had demonstrated himself to be caring, courteous, above all aware of those cultural and other differences that could have driven a wedge between them, if not carefully acknowledged and managed. So, the cynics were right in assuming he was a 'good catch' for her – but ignorant to the fact that she was a 'good catch' for him as well.

***

Henry had booked into a hotel just a couple of kilometres from the ferry terminal called the B&B Hotel, Ouistreham – one of a France-wide chain of hotels so named, he supposed. He found it very easily with the aid of Google

Maps.

"Don't suppose there'll be anyone at the reception desk at this time of night," he muttered to himself as he pulled into the car park, *"s'pose they have one of these automatic check-in systems, hope it works alright."*

He had some doubts as to his ability to navigate through all the codes and security systems he expected would be necessary to gain access. Still, the hotel looked all right from the exterior. A modern, medium-sized, squarish looking building, seemingly well-maintained, with discreet lighting indicating the way to the glass-fronted lobby round the side from the car park.

Picking up his travelling bag, he locked his car and walked over to the glass-fronted lobby doors. To his surprise they weren't locked, but when inside he found himself in a sort of cubicle with a second set of glass doors between him and the reception area beyond, which were. The reception area was in darkness and clearly unstaffed, inside the hotel there were just a few dim lights illuminating the reception desk and the drinks and snacks machine standing in the corner. No-one was about. However, there was a small keypad set into the inner doors, next to it a small notice which read:

'Veuillez entrer votre code personnel pour obtenir acces a notre B&B Hotel. Votre code d'acces sert egalement pour acceder a votre chambre.'

Henry fumbled in his jacket pocket for the piece of paper

on which he had written his reservation code when he made the booking a few days before. A four-figure number, one, seven, nine, eight… he punched it in, but nothing happened. He pressed the 'cancel' key and tried again… still nothing.

'Votre code de securite n'est pas valide. Veuillez reessayer.'

Henry started at the disembodied voice that made this announcement. He hadn't noticed the small speaker integrated into the keypad from which the voice had come. He was becoming a little flustered.

"Don't understand… already keyed the damn thing in twice…" he muttered to himself. *"How'm I going to get into this blasted place..."*

The disembodied female voice must have heard him.

'Pour des instructions en Francais, tappez un. Pour des instructions en Anglais, tappez deux. Pour des instructions dans une autre langue, tappez diez…'

Henry punched the number two button. Immediately, the disembodied voice replied in English:

'Thank you for your reservation with the B&B Hotel. I am here to help you. In order to obtain your access code, you must first pay for your reservation at the borne set into the wall on your right.'

Oh, so that was it, the reservation code wasn't the same

as the access code… Henry noticed for the first time the cash-machine-like thing set into the narrow wall between the two sets of glass doors. Turning round, he got out his credit card and inserted it into the machine.

'Please insert your card into the machine, then type in your reservation code to access your account with the B&B Hotel.'

The disembodied voice was now coming from a second speaker this time set into the payment machine. With its help, the check-in process did not seem too complicated, after all. The D.V. had a metallic but rather plaintive timbre, which Henry found quite reassuring.

'Now enter your credit card number using the second keypad. When you have entered your credit card number and your payment has been approved, you will be given your access code allowing you to enter B&B Hotel.'

Henry did as he was told. The system worked perfectly. He completed the process and waited to be given his access code.

'Thank you for making your reservation with B&B Hotels. Your reservation is now completed. Your access code is one, seven, nine, eight...'

'But that's the same number as my reservation code! I don't understand!'

Henry was very tired, he just wanted to get to bed. And

despite the soothing tone of the disembodied voice, he was becoming irritated.

"Didn't work the first time, so don't s'pose it'll work now..."

'I'm sorry, Mr Banff. I know the B&B Hotel access procedures can be quite confusing. But don't worry, Mr Banff. Now you have paid for your reservation, your access code has been validated. Please proceed to the keypad set into the inner doors and enter your validated code.'

Henry started, once again: this disembodied voice was full of surprises. It was a machine, of course, but how had it understood his misgivings? His name, of course, it had obtained from the reservation details. But beyond this it seemed to anticipate what he was thinking, what he was going to do next...

'And before you check in Mr Banff, may I ask you one more thing? I would like to know your opinion concerning how you have found this check-in process. If you agree, I would just like to ask you one or two questions about your check-in experience...'

Henry was very tired; he just wanted to get to bed as soon as possible. He was becoming rather fed up with this ridiculous voice that seemed to know in advance his every step, despite its soothing, palliative tone.

'...If you agree to take part in this survey, Mr Banff, you

will qualify for a 10% discount on your next reservation with B&B Hotels, which will automatically be credited to your account...'

"Oh, damn all this, can't you understand I just want to get off to bed?" Henry retorted testily. He turned back to the inner doors, in order to punch in his access code. But then he stopped.

'I am sorry, Mr Banff... please, may I call you Henry? I am here to help you. I am sorry if I have caused you some stress. I am sorry, Henry, I will trouble you no further and I hope you have a comfortable stay with B&B Hotels.'

Henry stood immobile in front of the glass inner doors. All he now had to do was punch in the number and (he supposed) he would be through, into the lobby, on his way to his room and the peace and quiet he so craved. But somehow, he couldn't do this. There was something in the disembodied voice – a kind of sadness, almost a cry for help – that held him back. He was fascinated by it, beguiled by it. He <u>wanted</u> to help. Somehow, in his mind, the sad, disembodied voice <u>needed</u> his help, needed some kind of release from something, and only he could provide it....

"Oh, what the hell, it's just a clever computer-generated system, that's all..."

His hand hovered over the keypad, but he still couldn't bring himself to punch in the code. He was furious with himself, but he just couldn't do it. In the end he turned back towards the payment machine.

"There's no trouble... no trouble at all"' he stammered out, hesitantly. *"I'll answer your questions about the check-in experience, if that's what you want. <u>Is</u> that what you want?"'*

There was silence for a few moments. Then, *'Thank you, Henry. Henry, you're right, I <u>don't know</u> what I want. Do you know what I want? You are a sensitive man, Henry, I felt this straight away. Henry, can you help me with what I want?'*

Henry was by now breathing heavily. He was fully alert, his dog-tiredness completely gone. This was a mad, mad situation: he was afraid and not afraid at the same time. But in the end, something about the disembodied voice made him feel calm, gave him self-assurance.

"Of course I want to help you. I knew all along that you needed help. Just tell me what I need to do."

Another brief silence. Then the sad, plaintive voice continued. *'Thank you, Henry, thank you so much. You do not know it, but you are helping me already. I can feel your goodness washing over me in a warm, comforting flow. Thank you, thank you, Henry. There is nothing more you need to do. I am feeling better already. Proceed to your room now in the B&B Hotel. I am at peace, and you will be at peace, also.'*

Henry was quivering with emotion, but it was true: he did

suddenly feel at peace. He keyed his access code into the keypad, and the door opened with a soft click. He was free to go.

'Thank you... thank you for releasing me,' he said, *'but... who are you? Are you real? What is your name?'*

Yet again, a brief pause before the reply came.

'Yes, Henry, I am real. But what is real and what is not real, I think that is the question? Yes, I have a name. It is Davinia.'

***

The next day was a busy one for Taniya. After dropping the children off at school, she proceeded to Queen Mary's Hospital in Roehampton where she worked part-time as a psychiatric therapist. She was there all morning, then in the afternoon went on to meet her Ukrainian friends at the Prosperity Cafe in Twickenham, which since the Russian invasion earlier that year had been organising and sending food and medical supplies to Ukraine. Taniya was actively involved in the relief efforts, and also gave therapy sessions to Ukrainian refugees who had settled in the area. Most of these were women with children, whose husbands were still in Ukraine participating in the war effort. Almost all of them had been through severe mental trauma, and Taniya strongly felt it was her duty to help them as much as possible.

For Henry, the coming of dawn was something of a relief;

despite what Davinia had said about him being at peace, he had passed a very restless, feverish night. Try as he might, he just could not stop thinking about Davinia. He would drift away into some dream about her - in which he was caring for her, taking her away to safety from that nameless fear that was stalking her – then he would jerk back into semi-awakeness, only to continue fantasising about her in one way or another. In the end, he had to admit to himself that he was in love with her. None of his dreams and fantasies was erotic, she still didn't have a physical form or a personality, but she was constantly in his mind. It was a weird sensation, making him feel elated, noble, bemused, purposeful and guilty all at the same time. For someone with as orderly a mind as Henry's it was all very disturbing.

After he got up, he felt better—not worried or tired at all. It struck him that this was odd, considering the desperately troubled night he had experienced. Fortunately, he could take his time, as his *rencontre* with the managing partners was not scheduled until the afternoon. He still thought a lot about Davinia, but not so constantly or so feverishly as before. He had a shower and got dressed, then dawdled down in the lift to the breakfast room for some light refreshment.

The reception desk was now staffed by a friendly young woman, who hailed him cheerfully as he went past in search of croissants and strong coffee.

'Bonjour, monsieur! J'espere que vous avez passe un bon

nuit dans l'hotel B&B...'

"Uh... ah, oui... pas mal, en tout cas... la chambre est tres confortable..."

The receptionist switched to English.

'Ah, you must be monsieur... Banniffe, if my pronunciation is correct? Un bon petit dejeuner is waiting for you, monsieur. We have croissants, and pains au chocolat, and oefs brouilles... crumpled eggs, I think you say? I hope you enjoy your breakfast at the B&B 'otel.'

Henry confirmed that he was indeed monsieur Banniffe, and that he was looking forward eagerly to the croissants and oeufs brouilles.

*'But you arrived 'ere late last night, monsieur, did you no*t? *I 'ope you found the entry procedure to the B&B 'otel not too ennervant... not too difficile, I mean to say.'*

Henry winced a little, demurred, and smiled politely.

"No, no, not too difficult... quite simple in fact, once I got used to it... got used to it, that is."

The receptionist had, of course, jerked his mind back to thoughts of Davinia. It was curious, Henry thought to himself, he had stopped brooding about her almost entirely since he had got up. He supposed that it was the daybreak – it was a pleasant, sunny morning – that brought this about. Last night seemed now like... well, not exactly a nightmare, but something that was no longer real, that had been just a fleeting fantasy all the time. *I must have been over-tired after my journey,'* he said to himself as he poured out his coffee, *'tired and susceptible; yes, I'm sure that's what it was.*

He continued to try and convince himself of this, although deep within himself he was not so sure.

***

Henry set off mid-morning from the B&B Hotel, Ouistreham, and was soon hammering down the A13 Autoroute in the direction of Paris. From time to time his thoughts *did* go back to Davinia and his experience of the night before; but not in the *same way* as the night before. Overall, he felt quite elated, fully in control of himself, and not at all concerned about his impending interview with the managing partners neither of whom he had met before.

"Huh!" he said to himself, *"I'm not going to let them bully me into doing something I don't want to do. I'm experienced enough at this international consulting game. Bet they've never set foot outside corporate headquarters, them with their MBA Degrees and political analysis claptrap and what have you."*

The managing partners (two of them) fully lived up to the expectations Henry had of them; youngish, snappily dressed in well-tailored blue suits and white shirts, exuding the corporate arrogance that marked them out unquestionably as graduates of ENA or some other elite, ultra-sophisticated *Grande Ecole* in Paris. Living, walking parodies of Emmanuel Macron and Gabriel Attal, Henry thought: they literally looked down their noses at him while scornfully informing him that his services would no longer be required by the Arnaque Partnership.

But Henry, who just a day before would have resigned himself to his fate without demur, pushed back against their cold, business-school-polished arrogance.

"Well now," he said slowly, *"of course, I'm aware that one or two of my projects have not turned out too well, recently, but that, after all, is hardly my fault. The environments in which these projects take place can be difficult; extremely difficult. Have either of you been to Trinidad and Tobago, by any chance?"*

The managing partners confessed that they had not.

"Well, as you would of course know if you'd been there – or even if you'd read some of the articles in 'The Economist' recently – that things are not going well, the price of oil being what it is currently and the political unrest in the Asian community you may have heard about. So there was a certain inevitability that our work out there would come to an abrupt end..."

Henry was bullshitting and he knew it, but he was rather enjoying giving the managing partners a little of their own medicine. And it worked; after a while they backed down from handing him his P45 and agreed rather to redeploy him as the partner in charge of administration in the London office. Something of a demotion as Henry knew well, but a role he would probably enjoy as he wound down to his early retirement and that nice stone-built *longere* in the Normandy countryside.

***

Mission accomplished, Henry set off with a light heart back down the A13 to pursue his secondary task, investigation of *gite rural* opportunities in *Seine Maritime* and *Calvados*. Davinia was by now less and less in his thoughts. When she did pop up in his consciousness, he felt only a warm glow of satisfaction. Had she been real, or not? If she *was* real, what had become of her? Anyway, whatever, he had done the right thing; he sensed that in some way she knew that she was safe now from her demons: and that in some way she was still with him, as a comforting and guiding presence.

She guided him in his evaluation of the various rural properties the hard-nosed, up-market estate agents presented to him for his consideration in Normandy. She guided him when he became hopelessly lost in the depths of the countryside, somewhere between Rouen and Pont Audemer. She was with him, and he was with her. When he arrived at the roundabout just outside Ouistreham on his way back to the ferry terminal, he spotted the B&B Hotel building standing just a hundred metres or so to the right, down a side road. But he didn't think of swerving aside. Davinia wasn't there anymore.

She was with him, guiding him, putting him unerringly in the right path. Just now, the right path happened to be the road to the ferry terminal, the Channel crossing and back home to Taniya.

***

The following day, Henry was back with his Taniya. He carefully explained to her how things had gone with the managing partners in Paris.

"They aren't happy about it, of course... they'd really like to see the back of me, as soon as possible. Of course, they're right in a sense, this business is changing rapidly, there's no place in it for an old warhorse like me. But I'm entitled to go out with a bit of dignity; after all, I've been with the firm nearly 30 years... not that it means anything to them, of course..."

Taniya, perhaps unsurprisingly, was more interested in the outcome of his property search in Normandy than the outcome of his locking of horns with the managing partners.

"Not all that successful, I'm afraid. The places they showed me were either too run-down to be worthwhile, or just simply not in the right location. And anyway, I wasn't going to make a decision about anything without you there to help me, was I?"

He squeezed her hand. He was genuinely proud of her, with her intelligence, her principles and convictions, and was happy to be sharing with her the outcome of his little escapade in *La Belle France*.

"But what about you? What have you been up to while I was away?"

"Oh Henry, nothing special. I have been at the hospital, as I always am on Tuesdays and Wednesdays…"

"…and I have been helping out at Prosperity, just like normal…"

Taniya sighed and brushed a strand of her yellow hair away from her face.

"There are some difficult cases with us at the moment, very difficult cases… yesterday I was with an old couple from Mariupol, who have lost everything, they just don't understand why it has all happened, what they are doing here so far from the place that was their home… Ah! That Vladimir Putin, if only he could know how many thousands and millions of lives he has destroyed with his famous 'special military operation'…"

Taniya paused in her monologue, clearly highly emotional and breathing deeply. She looked for a moment as if she was going to spit out all her hatred onto the carpet. Then she pulled herself together.

"And there is another case, a young woman with a six-year-old daughter, she came to me some time ago, and then again yesterday. Her husband was at the front, but

he has gone missing. There is not much hope. I do for her what I can, but it is so, so difficult."

Henry took a deep breath, and clutched Taniya's hand in a convulsive grip. He knew what she was going to say next.

"Yesterday, somehow, she seemed different. As if... well, as if she had in some way come to accept her situation."

"Her name is Davinia..."

A Most Transparent Gentleman

By Peach Berry, from her book 'A Bag of Souls'

"You found it," he said, as the door creaked shut behind me.

It was quiet, busier than I had imagined, but quiet still. A bar, a hovel of rickety bench chairs and tables, were scattered against the unnerving slope of a tumbledown ceiling, framing a short, stumpy wooden bar, placed just off the centre along the back wall. There was a man stood behind it, shuffling to the sounds of clinking glasses, the quiet roars of secret talk and laughter.

"Yes," I replied, shaking the droplets of rainfall from my coat, as the man gestured towards the free chair, opposite him. "I must admit, I had no idea this was here."

"I hope my directions were helpful," said the man, Mr Carter. "It is a well-kept secret; that's the beauty of a place like this."

"It's... quaint," I hesitated, looking around the room once more, studying the pictures on the walls, faded drawings of landscapes and town scenes, some so browned, cracked and weathered with age, they almost faded into the walls themselves.

"You're quite welcome," Mr Carter's eyes gestured across to the bar, his face never moving, not cracking once. I took this as an opportunity to order a drink, before the interview commenced.

I stood at the bar for a short time, careful to make little eye contact with the barman, or the other people, situated at the tables, there was discomfort in the air, something that tugged at the bottom of my skirt, that twisted in the loose curls of my hair. I felt out of place here, not used to my surroundings. I wanted to get the interview over with, as soon as I could, and get out of there. Whoever had heard of a bar like this? Hidden from the streams of bustling crowds in the city, the ghosts whose footsteps echoed above my head, as I drank in the stale atmosphere of the secret parlour. I had near enough fallen into the concealed entrance, had it not been for the gentleman, who had caught my arm as I slipped. I returned to my seat, a cool tumbler of gin in my hand, holding his gaze as the glass, dripping over ice, formed small pools in the creases of my hand.

Mr Carter sat, transfixed upon a spot by the front door; by a small window beside a cracked coat-hanging stand. His gaze was severe, his eyes glazed and widened in terror, I stopped short at the strange sight of a strange man, a stranger man than I had first, perhaps, judged.

"Are you alright, Mr Carter?" I said, not wishing to raise my voice.

"Quite, quite," he said, his body shuddering, his eyes darting back towards me as he regained himself. "I do apologise. A memory, I think."

"A memory of what?" intrigued, I pressed him further.

"My dear girl," he relaxed a little, his back pressed against the wall, as he readjusted his balance on the hard, wooden bench. "I wouldn't expect you to understand, it's just, I don't imagine you believe in ghosts, do you?"

I thought for a while, conjuring an answer that most suited my undecided nature towards these things. I had always given bumps in the night and ghoulish tales such little of my time and interest, being at one with the solid world around me.

"I wouldn't say I didn't believe, Mr Carter," I began, "I can't say I have ever had an experience to raise my question of belief."

"They exist, Miss Savage, of that I am certain." Mr Carter leaned in closer. "They say he haunts this place, the street above us. The previous owner. I knew of him a little. A very proud man, handsome and tall, friendly and forgiving. He died, a tragic car accident, some years back. I had never really thought of him, until..."

"Until what, Mr Carter?" I pressed again.

"Until I saw his face appear in the window, just behind you." I jumped as his eyes darted behind me.

"Impossible!" I scoffed, ignoring the sense of fear in my stomach.

"It is my belief, Miss Savage, that logic cannot always provide a suitable explanation." His face dropped into a crooked smile. "Say, how did you manage to find this place, in the end?"

A swift subject change, I sat my drink down on the table and readjusted myself on the small stool. Settled and, for some reason, wary of others listening in on our conversation, I began to tell Mr Carter the story of the man who had pulled me after my fall in the busy street, the man who led me to the hidden front door, the gateway to this strange place.

"He was charming." I began my tale, save for the memory of the cold chill that blew from the gentleman's mouth as he spoke in my direction, as if winter itself was encased between his lips. "You see, Mr Carter, I make little habit of coming out to meet strangers of an evening, I do not get tangled with the crowds, it is these busy times I cannot abide, the hustle as everyone fights to get out of this cold, wet weather."

"Do go on, Miss Savage." Mr Carter's tone held a tinge of annoyance.

"I'm sorry," I replied, rubbing my hands along my dress as I did so, attempting a nervous laugh. "Well, I suppose, what I was trying to say, was that I felt lost. Lost and overwhelmed by the rain, the bundles of people making their own short, sharp ways home, by the directions you had been so kind to write down for me. I tripped on the hem of my dress. A piece of lace trim, that had been snagging for days, had caught under the heel of my boot, causing me to lurch forwards, against the stride of the crowds, almost losing my grip completely on the unfamiliar steps.

I had little time to catch my breath, before a gloved hand reached out to mine, pulling me to safety. I felt the soft hide of black leather, the momentary glide as he pulled me up, before I took any notice of him. The stranger. I fell close against his chest, my hands splaying into his woollen overcoat, my eyes darting to focus on this silhouette of his top hat, as I caught my breath. The world melted away from us, for just a moment, as my eyes fell upon his face. A most handsome face, his smile was crooked, revealing the faint lines of yellowing teeth as he loosened his grip on my hand.

I immediately apologised for my error, thanking him for his efforts, brushing my dress down, with nerves as I turned to walk away.

'You are lost,' the stranger said.

'No, no,' I replied as I turned around to face him. 'No, I'm...well...yes, I'm looking for The Cellar Door, I am meeting someone there.'

The stranger laughed, his smile widening across his face as his soft, gloved hand pointed towards the stone steps that I had almost tripped over. I followed the point of his slender, coated arm, the long fingers encased in his glove, he smiled at me, to himself, as he proffered his other hand to guide me down the stairs. He muttered as he led me down the steps, nothing that I could remember, sentences or questions, they could have been either. The last thing I remember, I turned to thank the man who had been so courteous to escort me to my secret destination, to find he had vanished, disappeared into the night. Leaving nothing but the feel of creeping strangeness, as I made my way into the secret parlour, to you."

"An interesting story, Miss Savage," Mr Carter sounded somewhere in between bemused and afraid, "but you seem to be troubled by this stranger?"

"Perhaps, Mr Carter," I replied, replaying the moment my strange gentleman vanished from sight. "Confused, more. I remember he was ice cold, darting out of nowhere to save me as I tripped, it seemed almost meant."

"Those that linger on your mind, linger on this earth, longer than they should, Miss Savage." Mr Carter was cryptic, which prompted me to check my watch, conscious that I had not even begun the interview yet.

"I don't think I follow you," I replied, flashing a half smile, as Mr Carter sat forward, his voice quietening.

"A most transparent gentleman, a handsome face, a kind and mysterious demeanour?" Mr Carter began. "Your character sounds familiar, Miss Savage. Tell me, has it occurred to you, through the course of this meeting that your man and my ghost were made of the same stuff?"

"The face you saw?" I replied, eyes widened in terror as my skin crawled at the memory of his wintry presence. "The man who died in the accident?"

"Oh yes, Miss Savage." The wind blew around Mr Carter as another shadowy guest entered the building, slamming the door behind them. "I do believe you have met your first ghost, your first encounter with the Gentleman of Bridlesmith."

Paranormal Investigator

By Lisa J Rivers

Jeff

It had been a busy day for Jeff. He had to set up all the rooms in their latest location; a stately home in the Derbyshire countryside, ready for the 'stars' of the show, Cammy and Mike. There was also an extra person tonight, as they had just started bringing guests onto the show, to prove how credible they were as a team. Jeff hadn't met the guest yet but had been informed to make sure that all goes smoothly.

He had hidden speakers in a couple of the rooms, adding the usual sound 'mufflers' to ensure that the moans and groans of the 'ghosts' weren't too 'crisp'. They had to sound authentic, as Cammy liked to remind Jeff before every exploration. He tended to be clumsy, and as expected, he had fallen off the last rung of the ladder in the 'drawing room'.

He sat down at his desk with a cup of strong coffee and a cigarette, as he tapped on his keyboard to bring up video footage of each room that they would be visiting tonight. The cameras were much easier, as were meant to be there officially to record the team as they meander from one room to the next.

He clicked the camera for the kitchen; yes, there was no evidence of the fishing wire attached to the set of knives screwed to the wall. Jeff had attached the other end to a small rock under the sink. He made a note in his book to let Cammy know the location of the rock. He added a checkmark next to this note to indicate that he had tested this prop.

He clicked on the footage for the dining room. A large wooden dining table had a candelabra in the centre, and a Ouija board placed just nicely for the camera in that room. The team may have wanted to do a little table tipping tonight, which was quite a challenge with a heavy table like that. He swirled around on his swivel chair until he reached the props box that he kept close by.

"Ah! Here we go."

He pulled out some hydraulic pumps, stood up and slowly walked to the dining room. He glanced at his watch on the way over, realising that he only had an hour left until it was time for them to go on air. He increased his pace when he saw a black limousine appear at the large entry gates. Cammy hated it when not everything was in place before her grand entrance.

He entered the main hallway and trotted to the room at the far end of the house. As he approached the dining room, he stood in the doorway and mopped his sweaty brow, trying his hardest to catch his breath.

"This job'll be the death of me!" he chuckled to himself.

In reality, he did love his job, he just needed to make

some serious effort to live healthier, if he was to live past 50.

He walked over to the dining table and pulled one of the chairs out of the way. He lowered himself to the floor and used his shoulder to prop up the table at one corner, gingerly sliding a pad underneath the leg nearest to him. He shuffled along on his ass until he reached the next leg and repeated the process, ensuring that the wiring didn't get tangled up as he did so. As there would only be three or four sitting there, he didn't see the point in rigging up the other legs. He pulled back the large, old rug that lay beneath the table, a gush of dust wafting into his face, causing him to cough. He composed himself and pushed the wire and trigger point, a flat device, underneath.

He pulled his notebook out of his back pocket, unfolding it enough to make a note of the job completed. He gave himself a minute to recover for from this exertion before using one of the chairs to hoist himself back up. Felling a little lightheaded from the change in altitude, he leaned against the doorframe for a moment.

Regaining his composure, he folded the notebook and shoved it back into his jeans pocket and took a slow walk back to his surveillance van. To the left of the front door outside, he spotted the burger van that covered the catering for the crew. Yes, this was a top production company, not those online urban explorers that swamped the internet these days. He rubbed his hands in glee as he ordered his dinner of 2 greasy burgers and a portion of chips. He grabbed the food from the counter and continued his journey to the van. He could see that Cammy was waiting impatiently on his swivel chair, examining her watch several times as he approached.

***

Cammy

"Evening, Cam," Jeff greeted her cheerily.

She hated being happy unless she was on camera and effectively getting paid for it, and this reflected in her expression.

"Evening, Jeff," she mumbled, her voice expressing her mood perfectly. "What have you done to your elbow?"

Jeff hadn't even noticed that he was rubbing it. "Oh, I think I knocked it when I was in the house just now," he frowned.

Pleasantries exchanged, it was down to business. "Is everything set up?"

"Of course," Jeff replied, placing his food on his desk and retrieving his notebook. "In the kitchen, we have the knives: the rock is under the sink. The dining room has the Ouija board set up, and hydraulic pads under the two legs in the side where it is placed. There should be enough action for the candelabra to rattle too, and it may even fall over.

"Ah, good effect, that!" Cam replied, nodding her approval. "What names will you be using for the Ouija board?

"The usual suspects – George Beaumont owned the house around the 1700s, and most of the activity seems to be connected to his family."

There was a pause as Jeff flicked through the pages of notes he had made prior to these last-minute tasks. He rubbed his brow with the back of his hand and stepped further into the van to shield himself from the heat. Cammy stood up and moved away from the desk to allow Jeff to sit down and access his tech. He clicked on the middle monitor.

"In the master bedroom, there's a small crib…" he checked his notes in a different notebook. "Yes, yes, this crib dates back to the 18th century, which, as this background check confirms, was last used for a baby who died for just a few days after its birth. The mother, a young woman named Mary, found the child and was so distraught that she threw herself out of the window." He nodded at the window upstairs.

"It has a balcony, Jeff!" Cam retorted.

"Yes, yes…" Cam made him nervous. "I'll, I'll see if I can get more information to confirm this information."

"Ok, Jeff. So… the crib…?"

"The crib… ah, yes, yes. We have a small pump placed under the rocker in the far-right corner, so be careful not to walk around that end. I have it rigged to only rock gently, and the other pump for that set is attached to the rocking chair by the window. They will both rock independently to each other."

Cammy was starting to lose interest. "OK, next room then?"

"Yes, yes… the staircase. There's said to be a, erm…"

"Woman in white, Jeff?" Cammy interjected sarcastically.

"Erm… no, actually, a small child…"

"The one who died when it was a few days old?"

"No, no… it was his brother, Edmund, and he used to play on the stairs. He used to slide down the banisters. We've got a couple of the small balls ready to roll down the stairs when you stand on the first step. So, so mind that you don't trip or step on it."

"Noted."

There was a long pause.

"Is it all included in the portfolio, Jeff? Mike will be here shortly with the visitor, and we have to shut you away so that she can't see you."

"Erm… yes, yes…"

Jeff shuffled papers around on his desk until he found a folder made of white card, with the emblem CM on it. He handed it over, and Cammy nodded. She turned on her heel and exited the van, sighing and shaking her head. As she was shutting the door, she noticed that a second black limousine was approaching her. She turned round to look back at Jeff, who was sitting back in his chair, clearly relieved that the ordeal was over. She closed the door and put on her best fake smile.

***

Mike

"Mike! Hello! How was your journey?" Cam greeted him, air-kissing both cheeks.

"Pleasant, thank you, Cammy."

Cammy peered into the limousine. "Where is the…"

"Ah, yes, Shelley will be here shortly. She's just with the security team. Is everything ready to roll?"

Cammy handed Mike the white folder, and he opened it. Everything was typed up very neatly, a stark contrast to Jeff's notes.

"Master bedroom. Drawing room. Staircase Servants' quarters. Kitchen." He turned to look at Cammy. "No Ouija board this time?"

"Erm..., yes, Jeff assured me that there was one in the... the... dining room. I think it was a last minute set up for him."

"But confirmed?"

Cammy nodded, "Yes, Mike."

Truth be known, Cammy was as intimidated by Mike as Jeff was with her.

"Well, ok then. Ah, here comes Shelley now!"

***

Shelley

"Hello, Cammy. Am I allowed to call you Cammy? Sorry I'm very nervous!" Shelley introduced herself, extending her arm to shake Cammy's hand. "Sorry, my hand is a little clammy, Cammy," Shelley apologised, simultaneously wiping her hand on her coat and laughing nervously, before abandoning the hand shake as Cammy walked away, pretending to admire the architecture.

"Hello, Shelley," she replied, waving a hand at the house. "This house should be bringing us some treats tonight."

Shelley awkwardly placed her hand into her coat pocket. "Ah, lovely."

"You've not got a heart condition, have you, Shelley?" Cammy laughed.

"N… no, Cammy, I haven't."

"Jolly good."

They began walking towards the front door, Mike taking the lead. His camera equipment was stored in a large metal case, which had been placed on the console table to the left of the hallway, and he proceeded to check everything over before setting it all up.

The programme that they were recording was a documentary-style, with one person holding a camera and following the investigators around. However, there were also hidden cameras placed in every room for close-up shots. Mike ventured ahead of the two ladies as he checked each camera in each room.

Cammy wasn't a people-person; in fact, she often joked that she preferred the dead to the living, as they couldn't bore her with useless information. Mike always seemed to ensure that she was left with the visitors to make small talk, which was one of the main reasons why she was secretly looking for a new team to join her. If not to leave this current team, but more so to have someone else deal with the menial public.

"I was surprised when I was told that we'd get here so early," Shelley said to Cammy.

"Hmmm?" Cammy responded.

"I thought that paranormal investigations happened in

the early hours of the morning, when the veil is at its thinnest," she elaborated. "It's not even dark yet."

"Oh, don't worry, it will be!" Cammy grinned.

They walked into the drawing room and Shelley saw that all the windows were covered up with heavy curtains. She looked up and saw that the chandelier was switched on, casting prisms of light onto the walls and ceiling. Suddenly the lights switched off, and the room was in total darkness. Shelley squealed.

"Don't worry, Shelley, I'm here with you!" Cammy spoke in her tv presenter voice.

Shelley didn't dare speak. She didn't want to interrupt what she knew would be the intro to the show. Suddenly, a torch lit up the room. It was from Mike's camera.

"I assume you have been briefed, Shelley?" Cammy added. "We'll just be recording and can edit anything out that doesn't work for us. Just remember to not look at any cameras you may see in the background they are just there to pick up on anything we might miss."

Shelley nodded.

"We probably won't be able to hear you nod as we progress through the building, Shelley. You may need to do verbal communications."

"Yes, sorry," Shelley responded.

"OK, let's get started then. To any spirits in the house, knock twice for 'yes', and once for 'no'. Do you understand?"

Silence.

"Do we have any spirits with us tonight?"

'It's too early for spirits!' Shelley thought to herself, just before two taps could be heard from the doorframe between the two ladies.

Cammy jumped in surprise. "Bloody hell! I thought they were meant to tap further away than this!"

"I guess we'll cut your comment out then, Cammy!" Mike sighed.

"Well, I'm sorry! Jeff always puts the knocks through the speakers, which are over there!" She pointed her torch over by the window.

Mike sighed again. "Let's continue, whenever you are ready?"

Cammy nodded.

"You may need to do verbal communications!" Mike snapped, repeating her earlier statement to Shelley.

"Yes, yes, sorry!"

"3-2-1. Back on recording," Mike announced.

"How many spirits do we have with us tonight?" she asked.

One knock.

"Just one with us right now?" Cammy attempted to confirm, sure that Jeff had told them of a whole family.

Two knocks.

Cammy gasped. "Ooh, it felt like something just touched me on the shoulder!" she said. as she swung round to look at the doorframe, shining her torch nervously.

Shelley was quite excited by this. Cammy shone her torch around the room, her breath becoming shallow.

"OK, shall we move onto the next room?" she suggested.

She walked out of the room, continuing to swing the torch around in the dark, her mouth becoming dry. They entered the hallway again, and Cammy led them towards the kitchen. She paused, retrieving the briefing folder out of Mike's camera bag. She read the brief for the kitchen silently: *Knives flying, rock under sink. Stand near sink, knives will fall onto floor.*

Cammy guided the others over to the sink, feeling around for the rock under her feet.

"Is the cook here with us?" she called out.

Silence.

"Kitchen staff then? We know that Edward Beaumont Senior and his family had staff in the kitchen. Make yourself known!"

Silence.

She glanced up at the hidden speaker. 'Is Jeff asleep, or what?' she thought to herself angrily.

"We don't mean you any harm. Do you wish us harm?" She had set the question up ready for an angry ghost, as she kicked the rock beneath her foot. All five knives from the wall rack duly dropped on the floor, clattering loudly.

Shelley jumped and gasped.

Then, a heavy rolling pin appeared from the left of the room, hitting Cammy squarely on the forehead. She screamed in pain.

"What the hell was that?!" she screeched angrily, waving the torch around.

Mike moved closer to her and shone the light from his camera onto the floor to record the rolling pin weapon.

Cammy instantly flicked the kitchen light on to search for something to dab the blood leaking from her head. Shelley could see it slowly trickling down her nose. 'That ghost got her good and proper!' she thought.

"Bit of warning before you put the light on, Cammy!" Mike roared angrily.

"I'm sorry, **Mike**, I'm bleeding here. This wasn't in the brief!"

"Maybe you need to get your eyes checked then, **Camille**!" he replied, picking the file from the counter where Cammy had left it.

He studied it closely, flicking back and forth through the pages.

"What's wrong, **Michael**, can't find it either?!"

"I can't... It can't...?"

All three stood in silence for what seemed like an eternity; Cammy still dabbing her head, Mike rereading the info sheets compiled by Jeff, and Shelley feeling bemused. She wondered if this was normal for them behind the scenes. She didn't know who Jeff was, but it didn't sound very 18th century to her.

"OK, shall we continue?" Mike suggested, putting the file back into his camera bag. "I suggest we try the Ouija board next, in the dining room?"

"I guess so," Cammy replied.

The exited the kitchen, Mike switching off the light behind him.

"Action."

They moved towards the dining room. 'Hydraulics under

the two legs nearest the board, activated by the pedal underneath the rug,' Cammy ran through it in her mind. She sat down at the end of the table and indicated for Shelley to sit next to her, on the chair to the right. Mike sat on the chair at the other end of the room.

"Spirits," Cammy called out. "Would you mind joining us at the table?" She tapped on the chair on her left.

Silence.

Cammy was starting to get irritated now. She picked up the planchette and placed it on the centre of the board. Usually, there was a magnet under the table that controlled the planchette, but this was quite a thick wood, and she wasn't sure of the effectiveness. That didn't matter, of course, because she would simply push it wherever she wanted it to go.

"Place your finger lightly on the planchette, Shelley, and just let it go wherever the spirits wish to take it."

Shelley complied.

Cammy remembered that there was a Mary named as the lady of the house, so decided to start there.

"Mary. Edmund. Are you here?" she asked.

Nothing.

"Mary, Edmund...?" she repeated.

Cammy gently moved the planchette over to the word 'yes' on the board, but felt it pull towards the 'no' instead.

"Shelley, stop pushing it!" she snapped.

Mike sighed. "Cammy, stop breaking character!" He moved closer to the board to record the activity.

"But she's clearly pushing it."

"No...no I'm not, it must be the spirits," she said naïvely.

"OK," Cammy responded angrily. "What spirits do we have with us?"

The planchette pushed towards the letter 'J'. Cammy quicky racked her brains for an 18th century name beginning with 'J'. 'James, maybe?' she thought. Next it glided over to the 'E'. It slid towards the 'J' again but stopped at the 'F'. It slid down and then returned to the 'F'.

"JEFF, stop f... larking around! Either choose Mary or Edmund, or do something different!"

Suddenly, the table leg lifted up at the opposite end of the room, causing the candelabra to slide across, hitting Cammy in the chest. She swiped her hand at the centrepiece and threw it to the floor.

"STOP IT!" She was hysterical now.

Shelley just looked at her in amazement, her finger still poised on the planchette. Cammy was unravelling before her very eyes! This would be a great story to tell once she got out of here.

The planchette started moving again, and headed straight for the 'J', followed by the 'E", and then the 'F', twice!

The empty chair tipped over, and Cammy jumped to her feet.

"I'm done with him, and I'm done with you!" she screeched at Shelley. "When did you two get together to plot this attack?"

"I don't know any Jeff," Shelley replied.

"This session is done. Mike, sort this mess out. I doubt there'll be any salvageable footage from today. Shelley, come with me."

Cammy stormed out of the room, and Shelley followed her, glancing back at Mike.

Mike watched the two women leave and began to gather all his technical equipment, and packed it away.

***

Shelley

Shelley had no idea what was going on. She did her best

to follow Cammy around the large, pitch-black house. As they both approached the staircase, a small bouncy ball appeared from the top of the stairs, hitting Cammy on her ear.

"STOP IT, Jeff! You are sacked! You have seriously overstepped!" Cammy shrieked.

'This is fantastic,' Shelley thought, as she dodged a second ball.

The front door swung open, and daylight blinded both women for a moment as their eyes adjusted. No sooner had they focused on the door, than it slammed again, knocking Cammy over. Shelley dashed over to offer Cammy some assistance.

Cammy was in tears. "I never knew he hated me like this!" she sobbed.

She stood up, violently shoving away Shelley's hand. She opened the door again and dashed out before it had time to hit her again. Almost falling down the couple of steps that led to the driveway, she waved to the driver of the second limousine and he ran over to meet the women.

"You. Shelley. You can go. You've had the 'ghost experience' that you paid for."

The driver escorted the confused guest, who was already getting her mobile phone out of her pocket to tell the world what happened. Cammy spotted this.

"NDA, Shelley. NDA!"

***

Cammy

Cammy's personal chauffeur, seeing the commotion, returned to his seat in his vehicle and drove over to where Cammy was standing, looking dazed. He opened his door and then the rear passenger door and Cammy stepped inside.

"No, don't go yet," she told the driver as he walked back to his seat. "I just need to compose myself for a few minutes. It's been quite the ordeal."

The driver duly waited by Cammy's door, awaiting further instructions.

Cammy poured herself a large gin from the limousine's minibar and downed it in one. She'd never had to fire someone before, but this was more than deserved. She checked her wounds using her mirror compact, knowing that makeup wasn't going to resolve this matter. She poured herself another gin, but decided to wait until after the dismissal before drinking it.

She stood up and smoothed down her clothes, passing the glass to the driver. She silently walked over to Jeff's surveillance van and paused for a moment. 'This is the right thing to do,' she said to herself as she swung open the door.

Jeff

As the door opened, Cammy was met with a grizzly sight. At first, she thought Jeff was asleep in the chair, but when she shoved his arm, he slumped over the arm of his swivel chair and fell into a heap on the floor.

"Jeff! Jeff! Stop messing about!" Cammy yelled nervously.

Jeff didn't move. Cammy poked his arm.

Nothing.

She shrieked at the top of her voice.

***

As the paramedics left, one young man reassured Cammy that there was nothing that she could have done to save Jeff.

"It looks like he didn't feel any pain," he explained.

Cammy looked over at Jeff's desk and saw the two burgers and portion of chips were left untouched.

"How long...?"

"SOCO will have to confirm, but to me, it looks like around an hour."

Cammy glanced at her watch. It had been 55 minutes since they had started the investigation.

Too Much Candy and Gore

By H.L. Wood

Babysitting on Halloween night sounds like a bad idea, but I've been saving for college, and Jenny, the little girl I babysit, is the easiest kid to watch. Mrs Hastings pays me double rates on major holidays, so it's a double win for me. I get candy and their whole McMansion to myself to watch scary movies while Jenny goes to bed at 8 p.m. Her older brother, Tommy, throws the best parties in all of Lake County, an enormous bonfire up in the quarry while his mum and the other adults drink too much wine at the country club. That leaves me with the perfect evening: alone and free of all responsibility.

Which is exactly what I'm enjoying when the power cuts out, casting the house in a deep blue glow from the rising moon outside. Surely the generator will kick on soon, or maybe the breaker just blew. I remember Mrs Hastings said it's in the basement. A loud bang upstairs pulls my attention away from the dark cavern below the house. Jenny's small voice drifts down the hallway, drawing me up the stairs to the open balcony between the rooms. Most of the doors are closed against the cream-coloured walls, but my eyes catch on a darker part of the hallway. The shadows pool in the corners of the rooms a little more than they should, and my eyes adjust to the dim light.

Standing in the darkened hallway the outline of a tall,

broad man wearing an old boiler suit, one Jenny's dad used to wear for his car projects. The thing is so old it still has oil stains from twenty years ago. I'm pretty sure Mrs Hastings never had the heart to wash it after Mr Hastings's accident. That still doesn't explain, though, who's wearing it now standing at the end of the hall.

"Tommy? Is that you? Come on, stop playing around. You'll wake your sister, and then we'll *both* be in big trouble when your mom gets home!"

The person doesn't respond. Doesn't move. Just the slow, methodical rise and fall of his broad chest. I back away from the darkened hallway, retreating to the large landing on the balcony.

From here, I can see into Jenny's room. The plush pink bed is piled high with stuffed animals, and soft blankets lie in disarray, her pale arm hanging at an unnatural angle from the rest of her still body. A deep burn of acid rises in my throat, threatening to choke the air from my lungs, when the world around me bursts to life in a single instant. My feet move before the rest of me, hurtling back down the stairs as his large frame steps out of the shadows. Taking the stairs two at a time, I crash-land on the ground floor and twist around the living room doorframe, just as a bear-paw-sized hand seizes my hoodie. The soft grey fabric yanks me backward toward his chest, but I rip the zipper down and slip out, hitting the floor with a thud. I kick off the ground and scramble into a crawl, heading for the basement door I left wide open, now suddenly the most inviting place in the entire house.

I count the heavy footsteps as they fall on the stairs leading to the landing, each one accompanied by the whining of the floorboards above me. Blinking grit from my eyes, I pry the door open and tiptoe into the hall, the pale moon rising just above the trees. Grasping the cool doorknob, its squeak loud and sharp. I throw my body against the door as it swings open, pumping the blood from my head down into my calves to launch myself forward into the woods. A loud crash echoes behind me, booming down the stairs, pushing me deeper into the pitch-black forest

In the late October air, tendrils of branches whip across my face like icy cat scratches, obscuring my view of the ground in front of me, until I burst into the clearing by the small lake and its boathouse. Silence bleeds into the night, broken only by the slow lapping of water around me. A low, distant owl call makes my head snap in its direction. The feeling of being hunted pulses through my body, my heartbeat pounds like a frantic drum line inside my skull. But there's no breathing. No boots snapping twigs outside. Not a single rustle of a boiler suit. I take a cautious step toward the boathouse door. The lake's surface reflects perfectly, still as glass, not even a whisper of wind to disturb it. I scan the treeline. The forest is still; the only sign of my passage is the broken branches from my frantic retreat. I spin around in short, panicked bursts, searching. Listening.

The phone rings and rings, its shrill tone cutting through the night air. I hear the click of the receiver lifting, followed by the slow drag of a voice forming a question,

"How may I help?"

Before her words can fully reach me, I vomit my plea into the receiver.

"Please, someone's trying to kill me! I'm stranded out by the lake; I need everyone you've got!"

A chuckle crackles back through the line, freezing the blood in my veins.

"Oh please. If this is one of you kids up at the quarry, just know you're one noise complaint away from the sheriff coming up there."

Her light, almost cheerful voice stings like salt in an open wound.

"No! you don't understand. Someone is really trying to kill me. I think they already got little Jenny Hastings. I *really* need help!"

Desperation twists my voice into something raw, unfamiliar.

"Alright, now listen here," she snaps. "This isn't funny,

and wasting police time is a crime, I'll have you know. Don't you think the poor Hastings have been through enough? Just because it's Halloween doesn't mean you get to make them your joke. Good night."

The dial tone buzzes through the boathouse, flat and dull. The last shred of hope drains from my body as I sink down to the floor.

Wood splinters and dust rain down on me as the large man bursts through the trapdoor, just two feet from where I'm lying. His scarred, twisted hands shoot out and wrap around my bare ankles, yanking me down beneath the boathouse. The compacted wet sand knocks the air from my lungs as I hit the ground, my legs jerking violently in his grip. I gasp, sucking in gurgled mouthfuls of swampy air as I fling my hands toward the building's foundation. The age-warped, water-damaged wood crumbles into soft, rotten mulch between my fingers

His grip clamps onto my knee, then higher, wrapping around my throat with enough pressure to crush my windpipe. I thrash, my hands slap against the crusty, stained fabric of his suit. The handle of something sharp catches against my palm, splitting the skin open like an overripe peach. Gasping for breath, I latch onto it and drive it into the fleshy part of his torso. The handle slips from my grip, slick with blood. His own hand clamps over it, trying desperately to keep his insides where they belong. The frantic urge to run hits me in the gut hard enough to rattle my teeth. Instead, I pull myself closer, between his body and the wall, placing my hand over his and pull the blade free, the wet gasp that tickles my cheek grows cold in his next breath as I plunge the knife into his chest repeatedly, his body thrashes against me, knocking my head into the wall and snapping my chin up into my own teeth.

Warmth settles between my fingers as the boiler suit darkens to a grey-brown. His thrashing and groaning become sloppy and pitiful as more blood pulses outside his body. I sink to the floor with him. The pounding in my throat and head doesn't stop. Every inch of my body screams to lie down and close my eyes. My heart stutters against my ribs.

His choked voice drifts through the mask. "I just don't want you to leave... never wanted you to leave."

The sound pulls my stuttering heart into a thundering gallop, dragging memories from my mind, every single day, every birthday, every Christmas, every good report card or scraped knee. My dad's praise and well wishes bounce back at me from the man behind the mask. In the distance, the wailing of sirens and cars crunching over gravel register somewhere deep in my mind. The world is thrown into shades of blue and red, making the blood momentarily disappear. My shaking, numb hands rise of their own accord toward the mangled old welder's mask. Under the black darkness, my likeness stares back at me, colour drained from his face, red blood staining his lips as his breath rattles out in shallow waves.

"Dad? What… I don't get it. What have you done?"

The blissed-out look that doesn't reach his eyes settles on my face.

"The only thing I could think of to keep you from leaving your old man and running off to the city… just like your mother did."

The shouts of officers grow nearer behind the cabin. Everything will be fine soon. The police will find us, and I'll wake up from this nightmare on the sofa in the Hastings' overly comfortable living room, after eating too much candy and scaring myself with vintage Halloween gore.

The dull pulsing in my head pulls darkness around the edges of my vision, swarming my mind and filling my ears with cotton wool.

"Well, Dad, you did the only thing that'll guarantee I never set foot in this godforsaken town again. You made me a killer."

The knife drags from his ribs, and time seems to crawl to a stop. The good thing about movies is they teach you the important things in life, things you'll never need: how to escape quicksand, what to do if you get sent back in time, and how to survive the slasher, make sure they're dead for good.

"Goodbye, Dad."

It's the last thing I ever say to the man who raised me as I push the same knife he tried to kill me with into the side of his chest and up into his heart.

The burst of bright torchlight scorches my eyes. From the looks of it, half the police force is crowded into the narrow gap between the cabins. Raised voices and codes crackle over walkie-talkies, drifting above my head as I sink deeper into the darkness, deeper into the soft, plush sofa I so wish I were on. As the officer calls my name, I slip into the abyss.

The following weeks are spent in the hospital, with lots of wires, tubes, and beeping noise which make recovery from attempted murder quite the challenge. However, after three surgeries to reconstruct my skull and repair the hole in my lung, I'm finally allowed to escape the hospital walls, escorted in a wheelchair down to the gardens. The blooming flowers feel more like funeral arrangements than anything else.

The sun feels nice, even on this weak November morning. The people around the gardens seem to have clocked me. People have a lot of theories about that night. Some believe it was all an elaborate prank gone wrong. Others blame me for the entire ordeal. Some even say my dad was possessed by the vengeful spirit of the late Mr Hastings. But sadly, the sheriff and police confirmed my dad worked alone in his plan to murder

Jenny, me, and as many of the quarry kids as possible, to cover up my death among theirs, to keep me trapped in this town forever.

Being discharged from the hospital felt like a prison sentence far beyond what I deserved. The interviews and questions all resulted in a declaration of my innocence on the grounds of self-defence and heroism for the other teens in town. My home, however, has not fared the same. They slashed ugly words across the front. Inside, it's a boxed-up, empty shell. My aunt from my mother's side finally decided I'm worth dealing with, now that I'm something more than my dad's daughter.

The sale of the house is easy. It goes to some creepy, obsessed true crime fan who wants to charge people to see the 'murder houses' of Lake County, which is stupid, because no murder happened here. Leaving most of the boxes in storage for my trip to college. No need to drag old baggage with me. The need for a fresh start feels more important than memories forever stained with the smell of warm copper blood. My last view of Lake County is the quarry in the distance. Now I'm free to leave this place and never return...But in the rearview mirror, a slight flash catches my eye. I swear I saw a dark figure looming over the quarry's edge. I blink twice and it's gone.

ABOUT THE AUTHORS

Peach has written stories and poetry, particularly in the paranormal genre, since she was very young. Her fascination with ghost stories started at a very early age, when she would save up her pocket money to buy books about the paranormal and conduct ghost hunts at her primary school with unwilling fellow schoolmates at the supposedly-haunted 'treetops' house. She cites the work of Susan Hill, Stephen King and James Herbert as some of her biggest writing influences, though it doesn't hurt to be a die-hard heavy metal fan too!

'A Bag of Souls' is Peach's first collection of short stories, though she has several half-finished novels to finish and a whole wealth of creepy characters to introduce.

Peach hails from the wilds of Somerset originally, but now resides in Nottingham with her daughter, Daisy. When she isn't writing books or making up faces, Peach is a keen reader, dressmaker, collector of vintage and macabre treasures, drinker of gin and avid gig-goer.

Neil Pettifer is a dad of two living in Worcester with his wife and daughters.

He enjoyed reading, writing short stories and poems from a young age, probably spending more time than he should have getting lost in a world of his own. Neil found his greatest inspiration in his daughters; Amberleigh and Lilliana, who love getting into a good book as much as he does.

He has spent many years working in different educational settings and has enjoyed helping children learn to love literature.

 Kram Rednip is a former international management consultant and business writer with dual French/British nationality, who has travelled widely in the course of his professional career. He now lives quietly in France with an independent-minded wife and some cats.

His good friend Clovis Buckram (who makes an appearance in the Kram Kollection) says this of him:

"Kram Rednip? Oh, he's quite a decent sort, really. Can be a bit of a wimp at times. Fancies himself as a bit of an author, with all his scratchings and scribblings. Don't see him making it onto the Booker Prize shortlist myself, but you never know, I suppose."

Lisa J Rivers always wanted to write, and after being asked why she has so many cats, she decided that was where her writing career would begin! She compiled each poem chronologically, starting with her first cat, Kitty. Surprisingly, her obsession with cats didn't begin there, but instead, several years, and two/three cats later.

Since then, she has continued to write in many genres, including black comedy, short stories and Nordic crime dramas. She also writes under a couple of other pen names.

Lisa has 3 children, 2 granddaughters, and many cats! Born and bred in Leicester, she lived in Kent for 10 years and now resides in Derby. She is a fibromyalgia warrior and founded Green Cat Books back in 2017.

S.L. Saunders grew up in the northwest of England and has been lucky enough to enjoy the rural countryside, which has had a profound influence on her writing. She is passionate about educating others on preserving the beautiful natural aspects of the planet we call home.

The adventures of Ellie and the Underworld have been in the making for the last three decades, originating as a story told to her two children at the time (now three). Previously a teacher in further education, her circumstances now allow her to dedicate more time to her lifelong passion for writing, which began in her early childhood.

Pictures from her youth often depict her surrounded by books and sitting with her typewriter, painting a picture of her true ambition in life. Combined with her love for animals and the environment, it becomes clear how Ellie and the Underworld sprang to life in Sharon's imagination.

Richard Tyndall is an English consultant geologist and part time archaeologist who has spent the last 30 years working on oil rigs around the world and archaeological sites around Britain. When allowed home, he lives with his family - Liz, Alexandra and Phillip – in an ancient village on the Lincolnshire Edge, not too far from the quiet, historic market town of Newark in Nottinghamshire. It is this town, the surrounding villages, and their occupants, which form the inspiration for the fictional and timeless town of Aldwark around which most of Richard's supernatural stories are set.

H. L. Wood is at the beginning of her writing career, driven by a lifelong fascination with literature and the art of storytelling. Currently pursuing a BA (Hons) in English Literature, she combines academic study with an enduring passion for horror, the gothic, and all things wonderfully spooky. When she is not reading, she usually explores other storytelling forms of film, art, and digital media. Her creativity extends beyond the written word; she has also illustrated several book covers, blending her love of visual and literary expression. With dreams of graduating and working in a library, H. L. hopes to surround herself with the stories that inspire her most while continuing to write, illustrate, and publish her own hauntingly imaginative tales.

H. L. also created the image used for the cover for this book.

For more information about our books and services, please visit

www.greencatbooks.com